Not All Angels

Have Wings

To: Roger

Craig Georgeff

CRAIG GEORGEFF

ISBN 978-64258-476-9 (paperback)
ISBN 978-64258-477-6 (digital)

Christian Faith Publishing, Inc.
832 Park Avenue
Meadville, PA 16335
www.christianfaithpublishing.com

Printed in the United States of America

Dedicated to Carol Georgeff

THERE IS A village in Central Michigan much like Eureka Springs. For thirty years, a teacher arrived early and stayed late. Each day, she dedicated herself to her profession, encouraging respect, smiling at success, frowning at misbehavior, occasionally and privately crying over a failure, but always trying to share with her students her passion for reading. There were students who were the product of single family mothers, some who lived in dilapidated trailers set alongside lonely country roads, and others from affluent neighborhoods. There were students who were different, picked upon by some, bullied by others. There were smiling student aides and star athletes, coaches who developed character, and principals who supported their staff.

I shared my life with this real Carol for thirty-seven years and frequently visited her classroom. And night after night, as she corrected papers and developed lesson plans, I celebrated in a teacher's success or felt her frustration. I became familiar with the almost thirty names that were like family for those nine and one-half months. And just as I seemed to recognize the uniqueness of each, summer would arrive, and they would become less spoken. Then two months later, I would begin learning the names of another thirty. The real Carol lost a horrific battle with cancer far too early in life. The hundreds of books dedicated to her at her school and the local library signify that her efforts to share in a passion for reading were truly a success. Their presence illustrates that influencing others with her obsession for the written word established a basis for future accomplishments in so many young lives. Carol encouraged me to write this book and share some of the obstacles faced by any number of her real students. She never had a chance to read the completed version, but if it can instill in just one young mind an excitement in reading, I know she would term it a success. Maybe she would even offer it as a collection in the library that she now frequently visits in heaven.

CHAPTER 1

RICHIE RUBBED HIS tired eyes and listened to the sound of another vehicle. The continued revving of the engine as the car departed the stop sign at the intersection two hundred yards down the country road assured him that the vehicle would speed on by. There was no indication it was slowing, and besides, it made the smooth steady sound of acceleration, something totally unfamiliar to his mother's car. The sixty-foot trailer, set a bit too close to the road, shivered as the passing vehicle sped away. Then the sound was gone, disappearing into the blackness of an early November evening, heading west out toward Eureka Springs and then maybe to Lake Michigan further to the west.

He repositioned Volume D of the *World Book Encyclopedia* onto the middle of his chest, lowered his chin so he could see through his thick glasses, and started reading about the Dnepr River. By carefully twisting on the plastic frame, the two lenses now held together by white tape wrapped around the bridge, he adjusted the left lens to bring the words back into focus.

His mother would be angry when she discovered that he had broken his glasses once again. And then maybe, just maybe, the new white tape that held them together would go unnoticed. Little went unnoticed by her, though, and he fully expected that "How could you!" exclamation representing her display of concern. Then a momentary frown would make its way across her face followed by a pat on the head signifying that he was forgiven. And it was not as if he had been responsible because it was Clarence Goodfellow, the recess bully who somehow found pleasure in the act. This time, he had simply walked by and pulled them from around his ears and the bridge of his nose and, with a twist from his fat hands, left a lens dangling in each of his bear-like paws.

She would ask how he managed to break them, and he would make up some excuse about dropping them just like he had told Mrs. Learner, his fifth-grade teacher. The expression on Mrs. Learner's face when he offered her the explanation would be the same as his mother's. And as long as he did not waiver, did not offer one too many additional comments that indicated a possible hole in his story, the lie might be accepted. His teacher had gone into her desk for a roll of tape and intentionally dangled it in front of him.

Usually, that long revealing pause and the slow rotation of the role in front of his face allowed the itch of the white lie to build to a crescendo of nervousness that just might necessitate some further explanation and then a second untruth. And if she continued that unbearable silence with a questioning look, that could assuredly read the cloudiest of a fifth grader's mind you would be forced to confess to almost anything, done or undone.

But Richie was good at keeping a secret even if it meant bending the truth a little. Meeting her silent stare with one of his own, she had sighed, indicating she had accepted his explanation, bound the two pieces together, and placed the repaired object on the bridge of his nose. And once again, the world of Richie Small, fifth grader at Eureka Springs Community Schools, had come back into focus.

And there was nothing—absolutely nothing—that would have dragged the truth from him, not even the threat of the most extreme means of torture. Dealing with a crazed Clarence Goodfellow, especially after he had served another of his frequent after-school detentions, would be worse than any type of cruelty. It would take the threat of death or at least a trip to the office of Sid Glum, Middle School principal extraordinaire, to extract what had actually happened.

He could be avoided at recess, even in gym class, but it was the bus ride to and from school where Clarence was most dangerous. He had you trapped, trapped, and outside the watchful eye of any teacher or aide—first, because in the morning, everyone gathered at the two-way stop, the kids from the small subdivision and smattering of upscale and stylish homes all on the other side of the stop signs and Richie from the fading old modular down the street. And Richie had already learned that it was best to stand back on his side of the street and await the approaching bus, thereby avoiding the four or five minutes of pushing, shoving, and other forms of abuse, including one of Goodfellow's favorites—the knock on the back of the head.

But Clarence was devious. With that smile of helpfulness spread across his wide face, he would assist some of the younger children up onto the bus and wait for his victim. Then with a sudden push, a jostling bump, or an extended leg, he would do his dirty work. His victim, most often being Richie, would be left sprawling in the dirt, picking up scattered books, or tripping up the steps. If the bus driver caught a glimpse of what happened, Clarence would feign innocence, allow a wide smile to cross his fat and freckled face, and greet the bus driver with a salutation that reeked of insincerity. Somehow, Mrs. Driver seemed to usually accept the gesture as honestly offered and would respond, "Good morning, Clarence."

It might be a day or two before Clarence would again spring into action, especially if Mrs. Driver had given him any look of dissatisfaction. But for the ride to and from school, he had forty-five-plus kids trapped and, more or less, at his mercy in the long yellow tub called Bus 411.

His hulking presence would slowly come down the aisle, feigning assistance or a helpful gesture, and meticulously pick out a victim. And then with a hand as big as a ripe melon, he might administer the old "slug-oh" on the tip of the shoulder. It was a devastating shot. If placed just right, it brought with it an excruciating spasm that began at the tip of the shoulder, somehow slowly rode up the neck, started ears ringing on both sides of the head, and left the victim struggling to hold back the embarrassing tears that would term him a wimp or, worse yet, a baby.

It didn't matter if you tried to get a seat next to the window and as far away from the aisle as possible because while he was flabby, he was also big with a reach that could administer his meaning of fun no matter how far you could dip into the seat. Any complaint to Mrs. Driver was met with his look of denial, supported by an expression of angelic innocence that made the whites of his eyes appear as large as saucers. And there was no one—absolutely no one—who was willing to back up anyone that dare complain. Because if they did, it would just mean that the potential witness placed themselves at the top of the upcoming victim's list.

Another engine revved up at the stop sign, accelerated, and roared past the old trailer, leaving the aluminum siding rattling near the front door. Richie looked at the clock next to his bed. It was now after ten o'clock in the evening, and it had probably been a busy night, with truck drivers stopping off from the state highway for a late dinner, maybe a group from the bowling alley in town. His sigh attempted to control that growing sense of nervousness that accompanied his mother being away from home and his being alone, but it did nothing for the anxiety building up in the pit of his stomach.

He angled Volume D of the *World Book Encyclopedia* toward his face and read the caption under the picture of the barges traveling up the Dnepr and in the Russian city of Kiev. He wondered if Kiev was bigger than Eureka Springs. *It must have been*, he thought. It had a wide river running through it with barges on it. All Eureka Springs had was Tumble Creek that ran west from the underground spring that gave the little village its name. And in the heat of summer, you didn't need to take off your shoes to cross it, let alone be able to float a barge on it, its total breadth easily traversed by a single bound.

Even though he tried to stay awake, his eyes were growing heavy. He blinked and then gingerly removed his glasses and tried to rub away the feeling of heaviness building up in his eyes. He thought about his mother in order to keep the subtle power of sleep from overtaking him. She was a waitress at a restaurant in Mancelona, having to work two or three late shifts a week, and he did not like it when she was not home with him. She was a small and thin woman, even frail-looking, twenty-eight years of age. She had long brown hair that, when she did not have it fixed up and onto her head for work, flowed down to the middle of her back. Her hands were small and thin, but they were strong.

That summer, after they had moved, they had built the steps needed to enter the trailer. She picked up pieces of wood that Richie could only awkwardly drag across the yard and then nailed them together with a hammer that he could barely place on the top of a nail with the best efforts of both his hands. Someone once referred to her as wiry, but he only thought of her as awfully pretty.

Jennie, a neighbor from a half mile down the road, had made sure he was fed, had completed his homework, and was prepared for bed. After he was tucked in for the night and his light was out, she would leave and return to her husband and four children, the youngest who was just starting high school. Jennie had become a good friend to his mother, but it was her husband who always complained about his wife acting as a babysitter—an unpaid one at that, and he never made any attempt to hide his feelings, especially around Richie.

Richie did not mind when she left. With the noise from the tumbling of the lock from the outside and giving her a couple minutes to trek down the road, he would switch on the light next to his bed, perch his glasses over the edge of his nose, and begin reading. And anyway, he was ten years old, in fifth grade, and capable of taking care of himself, at least, some of the time.

Richie's father, he didn't have one. Well, he must have had one, he knew that much, but he had never met him. On one single occasion, his mother had told him that he had died during the Gulf War before Richie was born. She never again mentioned it, but the pain represented in her eyes when she told him was something that Richie would never forget, and for that reason, he had never again brought up the subject. Once he had heard his great-grandmother, in one of her more lucid moments, refer to him as wanting nothing to do with either of them—"Dumped her the moment he found out she was pregnant," she had said. That made Richie feel bad, but either way, the topic was never mentioned again. It was just he and his mother in a trailer that was owned by his great-grandmother now in a nursing home near Mancelona.

"The Dnepr River is the second longest waterway in European Russia," Richie read to himself from page 211 of Volume D. He had covered the first 210 pages in less than two weeks since just before Halloween articles about dairy farming, dance, the Dark Ages; stories about people like Clarence Darrow, Bette Davis, and Jefferson Davis; and descriptions of places like Delaware, Denver, Des Moines, and even Detroit, where he had been born.

The partial encyclopedia set, due to Volumes B, R, and S being missing, was his most precious possession other than his glasses. His mother had picked them up at a garage sale for fifty cents with a promise by the owner to search for the other volumes, and he planned to read them all, from A through Z. The chore was made easier, at least initially because Volume B was one of those among the missing and they had moved before the owner found the others. It didn't matter because there had been plenty to read about, first in Volumes A and C and now Volume D.

Volume D wavered and slowly fell forward on his chest. He resisted by blinking his eyes, pushing the book to its upright position, and concentrating at the print on the page. "The Dnepr rises near Smolenak in central European Russia." The words blurred, and the book tilted. "It flows southward for 1,410 miles to empty into the. . ." The book again gently fell forward onto his chest. Richie Small would have to wait until the morning to discover where exactly the Dnepr emptied.

CHAPTER 2

REBECCA SMALL, EVERYONE who had gotten to know her called her Becka, hung onto the wheel as the dilapidated vehicle bounced through the potholes that ringed the short driveway leading to her trailer. New struts, she thought, how much was that going to cost? She could change the plugs, even work on the carburetor, but struts meant a trip to a mechanic in Cypress Bluffs, a trip that was surely going to place a deep hit on her limited budget.

A squealing sound of worn brakes brought the sputtering old car to a final halt next to the front entryway. A single lightbulb, its ornate cover long ago broken or misplaced, shone brightly next to the door and indicated that Jennie was gone, having switched the light on as she left to return to her family further down the road. The venetian blinds in Richie's bedroom were ringed by a thin outline of a yellowish glow, and she suspected that his bedroom light was on because he had attempted to wait up for her.

He would either be in bed reading, his favorite hobby, or asleep with the pages of a book being a partial blanket. She fumbled for the keys in her pocketbook, got out of the car, and opened the door to the antiquated trailer she and her son called home.

She found him asleep, a volume of the encyclopedia draped over his chest, and his thick black-framed glasses perched awkwardly on his nose and over his closed eyes. New tape adorned the bridge of his glasses, and under her breath, she spoke the words, "Richie, how could you!" As deftly as possible, she tried to remove them from over his ears and off his nose in order not to wake him, but her effort resulted in a drowsy look up in her direction.

"Hi, Mom," Richie said sleepily, pushing his glasses back onto his face.

"Hi, ya slugger," she responded, rubbing her small thin hand through the black thick hair on his head. "You get some sleep now. It's late."

He pulled himself up in his bed and tried to shake the fuzziness of sleep from his head. "I'm okay," he said as he slid over to make room for her to sit.

She set her slight body on the bed, hardly making an impression on the firm mattress, and he laid his head on her lap. "A lot of customers tonight?" he asked.

"Yep, quite a few," she responded. "Most of the regulars."

Richie could smell the aromas of the restaurant food in the fabric of the plain dark brown skirt and pale yellow blouse she still wore, the blouse because of its light color having the more visible stains.

He sniffed the air and drew in the scents of what had become familiar as spills upon her clothing. "I smell barbecue sauce," he said.

"Wednesday night means ribs," she answered while tenderly stroking his thick hair.

"That means Mr. and Mrs. Tuttel were in and Mr. Evers and Mr. and Mrs. Johnson." He spoke with a sense of pride, happy that he could talk with his mother about what went on at the restaurant.

"That's right. Regulars on Wednesday night, like always," she replied. "I'm surprised you can always remember."

"Describe Mr. Evers to me, Mom." It was becoming a tradition that he chose one of the customers for her to talk about, someone for her to describe, and most importantly so he could keep his head in her lap and have her run her fingers gently through his hair.

"Oh, he's a robust man." She too participated in the tradition that included challenging him with new or different words. "I think he is a farmer over on the far side of Cypress Bluffs, ruddy complexion that appears to have seen far too many hours in the sun. His eyes are set wide and far apart, large hands and shoulders. . ." She continued describing the man he had inquired about.

He loved the sound of her delicate voice, something that he could listen to for hours. He hung on to every word as she spoke, knowing that there would be a type of quiz after she completed her description.

"Now the word *robust*, can you give me a definition?" she asked as she completed the word *portrait* that was creatively filled with clues.

"Like large and strong, someone like a farmer who works hard and has muscles, an active type of person," he responded, knowing that he was correct.

"I smell tartar sauce," he said, sniffing the waist of her blouse and hoping that she would continue.

"That is quite enough for tonight, big fellow."

"Come on, Mom." There was a small and insignificant plea in his voice, well knowing that it was late and that she would not continue. "Just one more?"

She gently began to rise from the bed, ignoring his appeal. "What happened here?" she asked as she took the glasses from his face and examined the new tape holding the two halves together.

Without his glasses balanced on his nose, she suddenly became nothing more than the outline of a person mixed in a brown and yellow blur. "Oh, they fell off in gym class. I think someone must have stepped on them." That was an explanation she might accept if she had not heard it three or four other times in the last two months.

"Richie, how could you!" Somehow, she spoke the words without an ounce of anger, and he knew that he was not in trouble. Yet there was that tone in her voice that indicated that she was not accepting his explanation, but it was just too late to demand the truth.

"I'll glue them together and put some more tape on them. Be as good as new, at least until I can afford some new ones. You get some sleep."

Before he turned over onto his pillow, he momentarily sat up, and as always, he felt the strong hug from her arms and the soft kiss of her lips on his cheek before the click of the light switch turned the blurriness into darkness. But he was very happy she was home.

After gingerly placing the glasses on the table in the kitchen, Becka Small emptied some of the tip money that remained in the pockets of her skirt. From her purse, she extracted some dollar bills and sorted and then counted the assortment of small bills and change. Thirty-seven dollars had been her take for a seven-hour evening shift. The money was better in the evening, the patrons somehow drawing the incorrect conclusion that breakfast and lunch, while surely less expensive, did not involve as much work for a waitress. Larger evening tips, combined with her hourly wage, meant that she could manage to eke out about $220 a week, that is if she worked at least three night shifts.

Working either in the morning or taking the evening shift meant that she could alternate, at least, some of the time she could remain home. On certain days, if working in the morning, she could wake him and have his breakfast ready on the table but be gone well prior to his leaving for school. On the other days, she would be able to get him off to school but would not see him until late at night, having departed for work long before he started his bus ride home. Since the restaurant was open only one-half day on Sundays, she could always spend more time with him on the weekend. But Saturdays were busy all day, and she oftentimes put in a shift and a half. She hated not being home in the afternoon and evenings but had no alternative, especially if she wanted to earn a little more, and they surely needed more than just a little.

She placed the dollar bills in a cookie jar high on an upper shelve in the kitchen and the change in a canister on the counter. Maybe if the dollar bills where a little harder to get to, she thought, there would be less temptation to spend them.

After washing her hands, she set out at making Richie's lunch for the next day. She would wake him and be gone before he left, but a peanut butter and jelly sandwich, cut celery and carrots, and a piece of angel food cake she had made over the weekend all packaged into a brown bag would await him in the refrigerator.

She wiped down the kitchen and reseated herself at the table with his glasses now in front of her. Cautiously, she removed the new tape and then what remained of older tape, and positioned the now separated lenses on the table. Using super glue, she dabbed each side of the nose piece in the gooey substance, wiped off the excess, and held the two pieces in place. While she waited, she looked around the clean but old trailer and realized just what type of life the two of them were leading.

They had moved up from Louisville, Kentucky, when her grandmother, Richie's great-grandmother, went into the nursing home over in Mancelona. There was no one else capable of looking after her, and while that meant that Becka would have to visit her two or three times a week, they, at least, had a rent-free place to live. The two of them, Becka and Richie, had worked hard to shore up the dilapidated structure over the summer using a good portion of the money that she had been able to save while working as a waitress in an exclusive restaurant in downtown Louisville.

Her car had made the trip but seemed to deteriorate at an alarming pace since they had arrived. First, a manifold leak and then two new tires and now struts and probably new brakes. Over in the far corner of the kitchen was a functioning washer, but the electric dryer's heating element always failed to light, and the clothes simply tumbled without any heat until they were dry. The television set worked, even though neither of them watched much, partially because the aluminum foil that accented the rabbit ears-type antenna still could only bring in two channels. At least, the furnace and well were both relatively new, but the refrigerator showed signs of wear and would suddenly hum and whine during an occasional cooling cycle, as if something had grasped its mechanical parts and was choking the life out of it.

She let go of the now reattached pieces of his glasses only to find that she had glued the tip of her index finger to the bridge of the glasses. She gently tore the skin away and picked off the excess dried glue. Retrieving a roll of white tape from a kitchen drawer, she deftly used the tape to cover the glue and the break, and again the glasses were one entire piece.

She had another uniform for tomorrow but would have to wash the one she now wore in the morning and begin the long drying process after she got home for work. She turned from where she sat and looked around. The assortment of old furnishings, odd lamps, and worn carpeting that faced her were hard to keep clean, but she managed.

Outside, an early November wind began to hollow around the trailer. Bails of straw surrounded the skirt of the venerable old structure and insulated the underside, but strong winds meant higher heating bills. She went over and turned down the thermostat, and it meant that she would have to sneak in and place another blanket over Richie's bed before she retired. She felt frightened and a little dejected. She was doing the best she could, but it was difficult. She got up, and using the light from the living room, she quietly snuck into Richie's room and placed his glasses on the table next to his bed. Then she gently covered him with the blanket. She peered down at him, a small boy, just as she was a small woman. No matter their situation, she loved him with all her heart. And now she would have to budget for new glasses.

CHAPTER 3

RICHIE DREW IN the cool sharpness of early autumn air. As he exhaled, a visible cloud of gray momentarily gathered out in front of his face like a small round cloud. After turning to lock the trailer door and safely tucking his key deep into his pants' pocket, he picked up his sack lunch in one hand and the satchel that contained his book and class planner in the other and ventured to the end of the driveway. From there he could see the bus stop at the four corners two hundred yards down the road.

The children from the subdivision of expensive homes and a smattering of other houses along the county road had started to gather in anticipation of the school bus that would be coming to the crossroad from the south. And there in the center of the gathering group, as if he were a king surrounded by his court, was the hulking shape of the grandiose Clarence Goodfellow.

The top of his rotund shape stood distinctly above even the older middle school children gathering around him. His huge body was adorned by the spherical shape of a bulbous head covered with a grand mop of red hair combed straight down his forehead. Even in the distance, Richie thought he could see the freckles that seemed to cover his entire face, blotting out the great majority of his pale skin. The seedy green eyes, which when focused on you meant you were going to be next, were separated by a wide flat nose that seemed to push his eyes to the very edge of his face as if they were in danger of falling back and into his ears. And as always, Clarence Goodfellow was the center of attention. It was not because the others held him in such esteem but because if they didn't, they would be the brunt of one of his pranks, the very worst being the old sock-oh delivered so effectively to the very tip of the victim's shoulder.

Richie hesitated and nonchalantly tried to look over the still uncut cornfield to determine if the bus was coming. It was always best to reach the corner just as the bus arrived. In that manner, he could avoid the taunts that Goodfellow always seemed to direct at him and then fall in line in order to be the last one on the bus. More importantly, he would be able to avoid the potential of his paw-like fist being placed on the very end of his shoulder. He could see nothing but thought he heard the slow deep whine of a motor laboring uphill from another stop still farther down the road, and so he started his advance toward the corner.

He arrived at the intersection thinking the bus would be down the street at another stop but instead discovered that a large truck was revving its engine before backing into the farm field. Now he was at the corner, in no man's land, conspicuously separated from the group by the width of the road and looking quite the fool standing alone on the opposite side of the street.

"Hey, Smallie." Goodfellow gargled out the words as the others focused on Richie. "Think quick." As Richie ducked, the corpulent antagonist threw a small rock over his head.

Richie crossed the street knowing that even Clarence would not be irresponsible enough to throw a rock at him at point-blank range.

"I ain't throwing at you, stupid," Clarence bellowed. "Just trying to scare off that there mangy thing following you."

Clarence picked up another rock. Pulling his gargantuan arm back over his shoulder, he twisted his massive torso and flung another rock across the road.

"Get out of here!" Clarence roared as the rock clattered on the shoulder of the road across the street.

Not knowing what Clarence was talking about, Richie turned and looked back in the direction from where he had come. There standing just past the stop sign on the other side of the road was a dirty, scruffy, medium-sized dog. It was so filthy Richie could not determine if it was brown, gray, or maybe even yellow. But as he looked at the dog, the animal seemed to focus her eyes right at him and tilt her head as if about to ask a question and then sat down on its hindquarters as if waiting for some indication of acceptance.

"That your new pet, Smallie?" Clarence asked as he bent over and picked up some more rocks. "Looks like something you might keep in that trailer of yours." Goodfellow threw another rock across the road, but the dog deftly stood, sidestepped the danger, and reseated itself as if challenging Goodfellow's aim and at the same time appearing as if wanting someone to invite her to join them.

"Needs a bath, probably just like you. You got running water in that there tin box of yours, Smallie?" Goodfellow's comment brought a laugh from some of the sixth graders as he threw another stone that sailed over the dog's head, the animal seemingly sensing it was something to ignore.

There was a sense of frustration on the fat redhead's face as the dog skillfully stood to avoid another missile thrown in its direction and again sat down. While the dog appeared harmless enough, even the king of the corner did not want to chance getting too close. Instead, he sought out another plan to torment the animal just as the large truck that had dumped a load of dirt revved up its engine and started up the road and toward the intersection.

Suddenly, Clarence's demeanor flip-flopped, just as it changed when he smiled at Mrs. Driver or Mr. Glum, that look of "I didn't do nothing" innocence on his face.

"Good dog. That's a good dog," Clarence said soothingly. The dog responded by standing, waggling its tail, and tilting its head while surveying the group of children.

Clarence glanced to his left and at the truck now gathering speed in the direction of the intersection. "Good dog. You stay there now. Not yet, doggie. You stay there until I tell you to come."

Clarence peeked out of one of his seedy green eyes in order to gauge the speed of the approaching truck. "Good doggie. Stay, doggie."

Suddenly, Richie realized what Clarence was doing. As the approaching truck gathered speed and as Clarence took in a deep breath to call the dog into the path of the speeding vehicle, Richie picked up a rock and flung it at the dog. "Get out of here! Get out of here, you mangy mutt!" Richie screamed out as gruffly as he could.

And then turning toward Clarence, and to this day not knowing exactly how he ever accumulated enough courage to do what he did next, he pulled back his arm and fist and threw the hardest punch he had ever thrown—in fact, the first punch he had ever thrown—into the very middle of the enormous hulk that stood in front of him. The blow trapped Clarence's attempt to call the dog into the street in the middle of his throat, and the words bubbled out as part-cough and part-belch, some of which ended up as spittle on his protruding belly. As the truck sped by, the dog scampered away from the intersection on the opposite side of the street.

While the dog was safe, Richie, more importantly, discovered that Clarence Goodfellow, the behemoth of the sixth grade, the king of the corner, the monarch of the playground, and the dispenser of the old sock-oh, was vulnerable that he could be had. For that single shot to the midsection revealed that the bulk, the size, the enormousness of the hulking Clarence Goodfellow was not composed of muscle or brawn or the sinewy strength that made the towering redhead the tormentor of all middle school students.

For Richie's arm, at least up to the elbow, had been swallowed up, had vanished into layer upon layer of pure unadulterated, mushy smooth as can be, genuine, a-product-of-too-many-trips-to-the-refrigerator fat. That's right, plain old fat. Clarence Goodfellow, while he might be massive, maybe even a hundred pounds heavier than any other student, while he was a head or more taller than anyone at the middle school, he was downright composed, at least, the greater portion of him, of blubber.

Richie retracted his arm, and it reappeared from the massive blob as if he had just pulled a spoon from a wet soupy mound of melting Jell-O. There stood the stunned Clarence Goodfellow, the aura of his grandeur having suffered more than a blow to his fat belly, the unanticipated reaction leaving him momentarily powerless. For some reason, he ignored Richie, but that only informed the diminutive Mr. Small that he was now scheduled to be the brunt of some future punishment, something far more devious then squashing Richie like a bug right there on the side of the road.

For now, Clarence turned to a fourth grader gathered at the stop and tried to temporarily save his reputation. "Think quick, Stevie boy," Clarence said as he simultaneously slapped him on the back of the head.

The fourth grader rubbed his head and stepped aside, but this time not as quickly and now not avoiding eye contact with his antagonist. Clarence Goodfellow was still a formidable object, but the invincibility had been penetrated. His paw-sized right hand could still dispense plenty of punishment, and no one enjoyed one of his headlocks— the one where he squeezed your head between his arm and body and awfully close to that looming armpit until the victim could smell the possibility of being stained for life from the odor emanating from the cavernous pit under his arm.

There was the realization of all those at the bus stop that day that big Mr. Goodfellow just might not be able to crush you like an empty juice carton with big strong arms. But there was still the obvious conclusion that his sheer weight, fat or not, could do extensive damage to anyone unlucky enough to be caught under an avalanche of it. At least, for that morning, the crown on the head of the king of the corner, monarch of the playground, ruler over all the intimidated middle schoolers, while still perched on his head, seemed to be in the precarious position of maybe, just maybe, being pushed off and on to the ground.

Richie did not notice the bus as it pulled up to the corner but turned and was one of the first ones on not really carrying where Clarence might be. Slipping into a seat behind the driver, he stared out the window and down the road back toward his trailer. He felt sad that he had yelled at the dog. He wondered if he had hurt the dog's feelings as he caught sight of her quickly trotting away. Its head was down below its shoulders, and its hindquarters seemed to bounce as it moved away, now seemingly wanting nothing to do with those at the bus stop. Under his breath, Richie whispered, "Sorry, dog. Sorry, old girl."

And just as his words reflected gently off the window, the dog turned and looked back at the long worn-out vehicle. It was like it had heard Richie's words, as if thinking and making up its mind. And as the bus pulled away, Richie saw the dog turn and continue to walk down the road and away from the corner. Then as the crossroad slipped out of his view, Richie thought he saw the dog turn up the gravel entrance of his driveway.

CHAPTER 4

"**M**R. SMALL, YOU** will bring your lunch back to the room, and we will work on getting these corrected." Mrs. Learner, Richie's fifth-grade teacher, layered out three sets of papers on the top of his desk, all of them displaying the poor scores of between 30 and 50 percent.

"Yes, ma'am," Richie replied in his always courteous manner, her statement catching him by surprise and scattering the thoughts of a mangy-looking dog trotting down the street and toward the driveway leading to their trailer.

She was not mean, just strict, and in the two and one-half months he had been in her class, he developed a certain respect for her no-nonsense approach. She kept the class focused and under control, not like some of the other teachers he had experienced in the past. He liked the uncompromising routine, even though other students complained about her being too tough. Even most of the others had begun to realize that she was not mean or tough; she simply expected them to get their work done, done well, and that expectation was something they all had started to appreciate. And she stressed reading, encouraging all her students to read, read books, magazines, newspapers. And while he would never admit to her how much he read, with or without her encouragement, the admiration for the printed word was something they shared together, even if it was his well-kept secret.

She was not a big woman; in fact, she was quite small. It was that uncompromising attitude, the fact that she demanded respect—respect for her and respect between the students—combined with an attitude that they as a class had a job to complete that made her size irrelevant. She never hollered. Instead, she simply broke off all communication, gazing out over the classroom, the deafening silence quickly pushing students into their seats, terminating that unnecessary conversation, closing desktops, and focusing all eyes forward. And in the back of their minds, all of them realized that the day she did raise her voice was the day they would rather be home with the flu.

Then there was the look that would cross her face, part-stare and part-scowl, that look without any words that would stop anyone in any of the fifth grades right in their tracks. When focused on someone for whatever reason, it would stop improper conduct in the hallways as quickly as someone could swallow, seat people back in their desks faster than their knees could bend, and drive even the thought of doing something wrong so completely from your head it was like a crow had landed on your shoulder and picked that thought neatly and totally from your brain.

He recalled a certain sixth grader who made it a practice to routinely belch his way down the hallway as if it were some great Olympic feat. As he rounded the corner near her room and again readying a world record effort, he came face-to-face with her, that look across her face. And now, suspended between his stomach and his throat was one of his premier burps, the granddaddy of digestive emissions that had absolutely nowhere to go. The rumor spread that he went to the office where they called for an ambulance, his windpipe almost totally blocked with something he could neither swallow nor emit. The rumor was not totally false because it was true that he was sent home that afternoon with a condition that ranged from somewhere between severe stomachache and a hernia.

Richie placed her at being about the age of his mother, maybe in her mid to late twenties. He noticed that a gold band and second ring with a small stone adorned the ring finger of her left hand, and he assumed she was married. He speculated she would be because she was pretty. Her thick blond hair was worn just to above her shoulder and always kept in place and away from her face by one of those plastic girl things Richie didn't really care about naming. She wore little makeup, like his mother, but her face seemed to be smoother and with fewer wrinkles, and he concluded that maybe she had less to worry about than his mother. She dressed neatly, always in nice clothing, something that he had seen his mother wear only on the most special of occasions. And while she was stern, he noticed that constant little upturned smile when the class was working, when the students were accomplishing something. That is what he liked about her most, the fact that she cared about what was going on in her fifth-grade class, that and the fact that they shared the same love for reading.

At the bell, Richie retrieved his lunch from his locker and returned to his classroom. It was not that he could not do the work, but it was part of his desire not to do anything that would make him stand out. Being the smallest kid in his class, maybe the entire fifth grade was bad enough. But a new student displaying a timid nature, with a Southern accent and thick black-rimmed glasses, and living in a run-down trailer that belonged to your great-grandmother all combined to put a big bull's-eye on your back, especially when out on the playground.

She spoke to him in a kindly manner, her eyes focusing directly on his face and with concern lacing her voice. "Richard, there is simply no excuse for work like that."

She pointed to the papers she had handed out before lunch. "I know that if you gave me a reasonable effort, you can do the work." She paused but with the focus still on his face and a kindness draped throughout her words. "I know that you can do this. Young man, it is something that simply demands that you concentrate."

He did not know what to say, so he answered her politely with a respectful, "Yes, ma'am."

She looked through her grade book as she spoke. "And you haven't turned in any book reports since progress reports went home. Have you completed any of the assigned reading?"

He did not answer her.

"Young man, I'm afraid that after school resource hours are something you are going to grow very accustomed to if I do not see some improvement."

Richie swallowed hard as if the thought intimidated him. He really did not mind staying after school for the extra hour. It avoided the bus ride home with the likes of Clarence Goodfellow and put him on the second bus home that left from the elementary school down the street. And anyway, no matter which shift his mother worked, he would be returning to an empty trailer.

"In fact, there is no excuse for these scores." Mrs. Learner was a little more forceful in her comments. "Let us say that you will have to stay both tonight and tomorrow, Richard."

"Hi, Mrs. Learner." The cheerful greeting came from Sarah Beamer, a high school senior who always wore a smile on her face that only complemented her cheerful demeanor. Sarah's attitude, along with her always straight A work product, had earned her a spot as a teacher's assistant.

"Hi, Sarah." Mrs. Learner turned away from Richie just as he offered his response.

"But Mrs. Learner, I can't, at least not tonight!" Richie's thunderous and untypical response surprised both him and his teacher.

"Well then, young man, I suggest you redo those three sets of papers." She looked back at him with what he recognized as that understanding gaze. "You bring those scores up to ninety percent, and then we will see."

She turned to Sarah. "When you finish, give them to Sarah. She can correct them. I have to meet with Mr. Glum and the other fifth-grade teachers." With the parting comment, Mrs. Learner left the room.

Richie busily set out at correcting three sets of papers. The math was simple to him, and he quickly corrected the fourteen of the twenty problems he had intentionally answered incorrectly. The spelling was no more difficult, and he deftly made the changes where needed. It was the second to last history question that created a dilemma. He recalled how the fifth-grade textbook had stated that at the time of the Revolutionary War, the state with the largest geographic territory was Virginia. But in Volume C of the *World Book Encyclopedia*, he had read that colonial New York had made a claim for all lands west reaching to the Pacific. So next to question 19, he answered Virginia, inserted an asterisk after which he said, "See explanation on the back of the paper." He then wrote the following:

> The fifth-grade text claims Virginia, then being all of present-day Virginia, Maryland, and West Virginia, was the largest state in area at the time of the Revolutionary War. This conclusion does not consider the claim by the state of New York that all lands to the west and reaching to the Pacific Ocean are part of New York. See Volume C of the *World Book Encyclopedia* under Colonial America.

After he finished, Richie grabbed his unopened lunch bag and gave the corrected papers to Sarah, who was writing out some afternoon work on the blackboard.

"Can I go down and get a milk?" Richie asked.

"Don't you think you want to see what still has to be corrected?" Sarah replied through that constant smile on her face.

"Oh, they are all correct. Well, maybe number nineteen on the history paper, but I wrote a note."

"Well, if you're sure." She motioned toward the door.

Richie raced from the classroom, opening his lunch on the way down to the cafeteria. Sticky peanut butter stuck to the roof of his mouth, and the fact that he had stuffed almost half the sandwich between his gums at one time did not help. Reaching the cafeteria, he fumbled in his pocket for the appropriate coins and handed them to the lunch room aide, hoping that the glob of goop that had balled up in his mouth could be made swallowable with a dose of milk. If he could get past choking himself to death, he could go to the library where he might find a book about dogs. It was a close call, the combination of bread, peanut butter, and now milk finally winding its way over the back of his tongue, slowly down his throat, and through the middle of his chest and landing with a wet thump in the pit of his stomach.

Sarah Beamer checked the math and the spelling and found all the corrections had been made. At first, she thought she should not have turned her back on little Richie Small. He probably had gotten into someone's desk and copied the corrected answers from a good student, possibly Janice Wright, the desk to his left. But it was the history paper that really attracted her attention. She knew there was not a set of encyclopedias in the classroom. She got up and went to Richie's desk and pulled open the top. It was neat for a boy's desk, but other than the classroom books and a couple sheets of paper, there were no other books.

"What's the problem, Sarah?" Mrs. Learner asked as she reentered the classroom.

"Richard Small isn't the best of students, is he?" she inquired.

"I have the sneaking suspicion that he just doesn't try," Mrs. Learner responded. "Maybe it is the adjustment to a new school. Maybe it is the fact that he is not accepted by the other students, at least not yet. I think something else is influencing Richard. I just have not been able to place my finger on it."

Sarah went back to the front of the room and handed the three sets of papers to her. "Corrected everything in a matter of minutes," she stated. "At first, I thought he might have copied from some other student." She pointed to answer 19 on the history paper.

Mrs. Learner read the explanation on the back. "I never knew that. Is this something from your high school American History class?"

"I didn't do that. I didn't tell him to write that, Mrs. Learner. That is the way he turned it in."

Mrs. Learner looked over the history paper and then the corrections on the math and spelling but returned to the statement on the back of the history paper and reread it aloud.

Carol Learner sat down at her desk and then peered in Sarah's direction as a big smile spread across her face. "Well, that little guy sure had me fooled."

Richie had made a mistake. He had exposed something about himself that he carefully had kept hidden. In his exuberance to get to the library and locate a book on dogs, he had let his guard down. He had revealed that he was smart, real smart. Once it was recognized by the other students, it would draw more barbs and taunts. Teacher's pet, four eyes, brainy-ack, nerd, or geek—he had heard it before. The bull's-eye on his back would be bigger than ever, even growing around his sides and then over his chest, so people would see it no matter whether he was coming or going. What he did not realize was that there was one thing different than what had always happened in the past. It would be Mrs. Learner who would recognize that he had hidden things for a reason, and it would be a secret that they both could keep, at least for a while.

CHAPTER 5

RICHIE HAD SPENT the remainder of his lunch period searching for a book about dogs. He had taken the book back into the classroom and hid it in his desk. At the end of the day, he inconspicuously transferred the book into an old leather black bag that served as his backpack and spoke briefly with Mrs. Learner about the resource hour. She confirmed what he already knew, that the corrections on his papers had been successfully made. But as she dismissed him, he thought it peculiar when she said, "This is the type of work that I will be expecting from you from now on, young man." The realization that he had exposed the true abilities of Richie Small had sailed right over his head. Instead, the thought that had consumed the remainder of the day centered on the mangy animal trotting back toward the trailer.

He rode the bus home, giving Clarence Goodfellow only a passing thought as his hulking presence lumbered down the aisle and past his seat. A light rain had sputtered its way through the afternoon, and as he jumped off the bus, his worn tennis shoes slipped through the accumulation of mud that rimmed the pavement of the road. He crossed the intersection and scurried down the edge of the pavement leading toward his home. Turning up the driveway he hoped to see the dog sitting in front of the trailer, but he saw nothing more than the gathering of small puddles of water between the tufts of grass that dotted the front yard.

Stepping up onto the small wooden porch, he searched the empty yard and out to the tall stalks of corn in the fields that surrounded the small patch of ground on which the trailer sat. There was no indication of any dog. As he reached into the bottom of his pants' pocket to retrieve the key, he looked down onto the wooden deck. A set of muddy paw prints of a dog were in the process of being washed away by the rain. Suddenly, he felt a strange flutter in the middle of his chest, a sense of excitement. He turned and studied the patches of dirt interspersed in the grass, especially along the gravel driveway. The light rain had flattened the soil into unbroken layers of mud without a print being in sight.

"Lady. Come here, Lady!" As soon as he spoke the words, he wondered why he had chosen that name, a girl name for a dog at that, and there was no good reason for why he had. He sat down on the porch and waited, hoping the dog would appear from the stands of corn. As the drizzle continued, he felt the water collect on his thick black hair and then run down onto his forehead, and he knew it was time to go in.

There was a note on the table from Jennie informing him that his mother had left a message with her. With two waitresses out with the flu, she had the opportunity to work two shifts, both today and tomorrow, which meant that she would again be home after Richie was in bed. Jennie had left a warm meal on the table, but her note also explained that she and her husband would be gone for a couple of days visiting their oldest son at Ferris State.

Richie removed the tin foil from the still warm dish and peered into pork roast simmering in potatoes and carrots and all swimming in light-colored gravy. He tore off some paper towel to serve as a napkin and began picking through the dish when he suddenly realized that while he might not be too hungry, the dog would be. He got up, opened the refrigerator, and rummaged through what little there was available. He settled on the carton of milk and some white bread on the counter, tearing up two slices and placing them in a plastic cottage cheese container and then floating them in milk. Opening the front door of the trailer, he placed the container where he had seen the paw prints and from where he could sit in a chair and conveniently glance out the window that overlooked the porch. He retrieved his dish of pot roast and positioned himself in the chair, hoping to see the dog.

Thirty minutes had passed while Richie ate, but there was no dog. He finished and got up to wash off the plate and the utensils and then checked the container through the window. The bread now was swimming in milk and rainwater, the continuous drizzle on the uncovered porch starting to slowly fill the container. Richie did some of his assigned chores while continuously checking the bowl. Finally, he opened his satchel and extracted his homework and the book on dogs. Quickly finishing his work, he rechecked the porch and then settled into the contents of the book.

He searched the Table of Contents and found a section on Labrador Retrievers, having reached the conclusion in the library that the dog most resembled that breed. He read that Labrador Retrievers were hunting dogs, at home in the water as they were on land. Either black, yellow, or chocolate, the dog at the bus stop was obviously yellow under the filthy matting of dirt that covered her coat. The book further designated the breed of dogs as either being American Labradors or British Labradors. The differences between the two involved the shape of the head and bodies. The British Labrador had a shorter snout and shorter legs than its American cousin and also displayed a stockier body and more width between the shoulders. Richie studied the photographs and determined that the mangy and dirt-covered dog at the bus stop was indeed a British Labrador, even though its body was leaner than those in the pictures, probably because it needed to be fed.

Richie breezed through the pages of the book, devouring the information about the history of the breed and their use as dogs for hunting birds, especially waterfowl. There was information about their even temperament, their ability to be trained for such special skills as seeing eye dogs for the blind and special need dogs for people confined to wheelchairs. Their incredible sense of smell had them being trained for all types of special assignments with police agencies and the military. One section was devoted to their gentle behavior and adaptability around children and other animals, not only dogs but also cats and farm animals. As he finished each section of the book, Richie rechecked the porch only to find the bread becoming more waterlogged than soaked in milk and with no sign of any dog being present.

Finally, he realized that it was growing late, and he closed the book, took his shower, and laid out his only other set of clothes for the next school day. He placed his used set of school clothes atop the washer, knowing that his mother did not want him doing the wash. While she might have some type of hang-up about washing whites and colored fabrics together, he simply did not know what difference it made as long as they all came out clean. While it was a chore that he knew he could do, his mother was very specific about this rule, so he did as she instructed.

After checking the container one more time, he slipped into bed with the book on dogs, hoping to stay awake until his mother came home. After reading only two pages, he suddenly realized that the first thing his mother would see at the front door was the plastic cheese container with food in it. A dog was something they had never discussed, but he thought there was no sense in making her think about the possibility.

He got out of bed and went to the porch to retrieve the water-downed container, dump out the contents, and place a clean container back in the cupboard. But there on the porch was an empty cottage cheese container, licked dry, with only a splattering of several raindrops having accumulated in the bottom. He peered out into the wet darkness of the night. The yard was empty, but there on the porch next to the dish were two muddy prints made by the paws of a dog. Richie picked up the container and returned it to the kitchen. He realized that she was gone, gone for now, because she was not ready to meet. But he would go to bed knowing that she was not hungry, and that made him feel real good.

CHAPTER 6

CLARENCE GOODFELLOW HAD schemed and plotted the entire day, continuing his planning throughout the evening. He had slept with his eyes wide open, like giant broken eggs in the freckled round pan of a face. The next morning, he arose with a strategy that would surely gain the revenge he desired to rain down upon Richie Small. He had studied the elements, the fact that it had rained throughout the previous day with two additional downpours during the night, the combined rainfall surely forming deep puddles along the shoulders of all the country roads. And it was Friday when the students in the middle school would attend their extracurricular classes like art, music, and band, the band members carrying their instruments to school in cumbersome cases.

Clarence knew how Richie always tried to arrive late at the bus stop, and he included that fact as part of his plan. He measured and calculated in his devious mind where the bus always stopped. He pictured how he would place his humongous tuba case on the shoulder of the road at the edge of the ditch that would be filled with the swirling dirty water running out from the recently harvested and cultivated farm fields. And as Richie Small approached gingerly and stepped around the puddles along the shoulder of the road and Bus 411 accelerated from the stop up and over the knoll to the west, Clarence waited in gleeful anticipation of getting his revenge.

It had worked out just as he had planned. If given the opportunity, Richie would always try to be last, avoiding the brunt of Goodfellow's intentions. This morning was no different. And as Clarence Goodfellow got on the bus just before the approaching Richie Small, he initiated his scheme.

"Oh, I forgot my tuba!" Clarence bellowed out in Mrs. Driver's direction in an attempt to conceal his true intentions. And being too large to turn around on the steps of the school bus, the overly rotund Goodfellow backed down the steps in the doorway of the bus.

There could be nothing worse than coming face-to-face with the derriere of Clarence Goodfellow. It was gigantic, blotting out the entire doorway of the bus, the figure of Mrs. Driver, and the two seats immediately behind her. It retreated backward in his direction, jiggling and gyrating as it twisted down the steps, a seething mass of the worse kind of fat, rear-end blubber. Richie backpedaled as he faced a cascading avalanche of Goodfellow butt. And as he did, there at the heels of his shoes and behind him was the massive, almost immovable presence of the tuba case.

Richie pitched backward over the case, onto the edge of the slimy ditch, and then down its muddy bank and into the flow of dirty water. He finally came to rest in the mucky bottom with the water in the ditch swirling up to the middle of his chest.

"Oh my!" Goodfellow bellowed, still not having fully turned around. "Richie Small has fallen. Are you all right, Richie?" The sympathy in Goodfellow's voice was calculated only for Mrs. Driver's benefit.

Richie clawed his way back up the muddy bank as the mass of Clarence Goodfellow cleared the doorway and fully turned around.

"Here, let me help you." The heavy protagonist extended his stubby paw of a hand.

"Goodfellow, get on the bus! I've just about had it with your antics!" Mrs. Driver's statement was surprisingly laced with a realistic view of how Clarence always acted.

"It was an accident!" Clarence exclaimed as his massive hulk headed back into the bus, barely able to fit through the doorway with or without his tuba case.

Mrs. Driver turned off the ignition. "Goodfellow, you sit there, right behind me. I am going to have Mr. Glum deal with you when we get to school."

"Richie, are you okay?" she asked as he regained the level roadside shoulder totally soaked and mud-covered.

Richie nodded his head yes. He attempted to control himself and not follow Clarence into the bus and harpoon the fat beast with another fist to the blubber of his midsection. At least, he thought, Mrs. Driver recognized what had happened, and Principal Glum would dole out some type of punishment.

"You can't go to school like that," Mrs. Driver said. "Get on and I'll drive you home."

"It's okay," Richie responded. "I just live right over there." He motioned over the top of the bus. "I can walk."

"You go right home and get out of those clothes and then have your mother or someone bring you in to school."

Richie again nodded yes as Mrs. Driver pulled the lever to close the door, and the bus slowly pulled away.

As the mass of yellow pulled forward and he could step from the shoulder to cross the street, Richie's eyes instantly locked on the Labrador sitting on the opposite side of the road. The dog's head was tilted, and its ears pricked upward as if it were studying Richie and wondering how a boy could be so mud-covered. Richie moved across the pavement, and the dog's tail began to swish from side to side, even though it was still seated. Richie extended his hand as he approached, and the dog stood and carefully smelled the back of his hand, her tail still swishing the air from side to side with almost a snapping action.

"Good girl," Richie said in a soothing voice as he patted the dog on the head.

The dog sniffed the air around them as if still wondering about the boy in front of her. And as Richie dropped his hand from the dog's head, the animal gave the back of his hand a lick and then fell in place next to him as they walked back toward the trailer.

CHAPTER 7

T HE TWO ITEMS that concerned him most were his glasses and the key. The thick black-rimmed spectacles had remained affixed securely to the bridge of his nose, the backs of the frames wrapped snugly around his ears. He tried to insert his mud-covered hand into the sopping wet pocket of his pants, but the combination of mud and water snagged his fingertips as they attempted to pry the top of the pocket open. Finally, he wiggled his fingers down the pocket until one of his fingers came in contact with metal. He worked a second finger around the key, managed to slowly pull it to the top of the pocket, allowed it to squirt out into the palm of his other hand, and then fumbled it into the lock in the door.

Before turning the handle, he looked down at the dog still beside him seated on her haunches. He suspected that he was even more scruffy and filthy than the animal that examined him with a sense of curiosity. He turned the handle, and the dog's head slanted toward him with obvious anticipation and then with the same look at the opening door. Finally, she refocused her black round eyes right into the lenses of Richie's glasses, tilted her head, and offered an expression that stated that there was no way she wanted to remain outside.

"Okay, girl, so you want to come in." He spoke in a soothing voice, and the animal responded with a wagging of the tail that swished across the wood of the deck, sweeping water from the puddles that had accumulated on the planking.

"If you go in, you stay with me. I have enough of a mess to clean up without you wandering all over the trailer," Richie stated in a tone of voice that was meant to warn the dog but really wondering if she understood.

The dog rose from its hindquarters, barked once, and slapped her tail from side to side.

"You behave now."

The dog responded with a loud bark.

Richie stepped through the open door, and the dog stepped in and stood beside him. "Stay."

Richie commanded, and surprisingly the dog sat on the mat inside the trailer doorway as Richie took off his shoes and left them on the mat. Richie gingerly walked through the living room, his saturated socks creating small puddles of water with every step on the worn carpeting. Turning into the kitchen and toward the almost antique washer and dryer near the rear door, his wet socks slipped along the linoleum, and he almost skated to the wash machine. He took off his clothes placed them into the washer, added soap, and, with a twist of the dial, started filling the tub with water. He rinsed some of the mud from his hands under the flow of the water feeding into the tub, grabbed a towel, and draped it around his body.

Retracing his steps through the kitchen and living room, he noticed that the dog still sat on the mat. She tilted her head and pricked up her ears, transfixed on his every movement, one ear or the other twitching with every sound he made. He was about to step down the hallway to the bathroom when he recalled that the dog was just as dirty as he. Unless he took on the task of cleaning her up, she would be relegated to the mat at the doorway.

He looked back at the puddles of dirty water that had dripped from his clothing. There would be a major mess for him to clean up, dog or no dog. If the dog were to remain in the house, there was only one alternative. That was to clean her up, and as best he could conclude, that meant giving her a bath.

"Come here." The dog immediately stood and walked across the room to his side, its tail starting that now anticipated slapping from side to side and her eyes focused squarely in his face.

"You ever had a bath, dog?" The dog tilted its head. "Well, I guess we'll find out." Richie focused on the penetrating stare of the dog. "Let's go." And with that, the dog followed him into the bathroom.

It had taken Richie an hour to first bathe himself and then get the dog into the tub and again rinse himself off in the shower and then dry them both. Drying the dog was not as difficult as he thought, seemingly the water and soap effectively washing her off without totally penetrating a coat that was made of several layers of hair. They both emerged clean with the dog smelling of the shampoo that his mother used to wash her hair. It had seemed to have been the best alternative, and at least, it resulted in the most suds.

After having spent an hour getting the mud and dirt off him and then the dog and then wiping up the mess in the living room and washing the kitchen floor, Richie suddenly found himself not only exhausted but also hungry. He went to the kitchen, took the clothes from the washer, placed them in the dryer, and turned the timer on the dryer to "air," the only cycle that functioned. He then turned his attention to food.

He retrieved bread for toast and eventually buttered the darker side. Sitting at the small table in the kitchen, he watched as the dog reacted, intensely following the bread from the plate to his mouth. Each movement of his hand with food in its grasp became the center of the dog's total concern. He wondered if toast was something a dog liked to eat. Richie broke off a quarter of the second slice, held it out, and with a quick motion, the dog cleanly separated the bread from his fingertips with one graceful snap of its mouth.

"Guess you're hungry, girl."

Richie patted the dog on the head and fed her the rest of the bread and then placed two more slices in the toaster, one for himself and one for the dog. He opened the refrigerator and pulled out the plastic milk jug. Pouring a glass of milk for himself, he thought the dog might be thirsty and used an empty margarine container to offer the dog water. The animal's attention was focused on the toaster, and with the distinctive snap of the bread being ejected, the dog's tail began to wag. After eating an entire piece of toast, the dog turned to the margarine container and lapped out half the water with its tongue.

Richie had no intention of returning to school, his one pair of school pants now in the dryer on the air cycle and the other still in the dirty clothes hamper next to the washer. Even worse, his only pair of shoes were totally saturated. Instead, he turned on the television, adjusted the tin foil on the rabbit ear antenna, and was able to bring in a good picture of *The Price Is Right*. The dog sat at the side of the chair and eventually lay down next to him. As he watched Bob Barker give away things like an oak dining room set, a new car, and then a trip to London, he gently dropped his hand down the side of the chair and felt the soft fine fur on the back of the dog's neck. Then he lifted his hand away and suspended it over the dog. He felt the wet nudge of the dog's nose, and the nudging continued until he again started scratching along the top of the dog's head. And Richie liked knowing that the animal wanted to be petted.

He half-expected his mother to come home between her two shifts but remembered how she said something about taking the car in to have the brakes checked. It was a long day for her, leaving just after getting his breakfast and not returning until after ten o'clock in the evening, maybe eleven o'clock or later since it was Friday. He contemplated what he could do to help her around the house. He turned off the television during *The Price Is Right* second show-case and began cleaning up around the house, washing the dishes, and then going to clean his room.

Every time he moved, the dog went with him. She positioned herself next to him as he stood on the stool next to the sink, peered up at him as he checked the dryer, and then went into his bedroom with him, tracing his every move with her constant gaze. Finally, he grabbed the book about dogs and lay down on his bed.

He had only finished two or three pages when, with an almost effortless bound, the dog leaped up onto the bed and looked at Richie with what seemed to be a questioning gaze. Soliciting no objection from the boy, the dog comfortably positioned herself at his feet and placed her head and one paw over his ankle. Richie did not object. And from over the top of the book as he read, he watched as her eyes at first studied him, started to blink, closed for several seconds, and then remained closed. And with a long sigh fluttering the edge of whatever lips a dog had, she appeared to be asleep.

Richie liked the feeling of the dog's head and paw on his leg and the rhythmic breathing that slightly bounced through the mattress and could be felt along the back side of his leg. Comfortably settling into reading the book, he would, from time to time, lower the book and observe his new friend. The dog slept soundly at his feet. At least, that is what he thought. But every so often, when the book was raised and the boy could not see her, she would open her eyes to see the boy, assuring herself that everything was right.

They spent the rest of the day reading, doing chores, and going outside for the dog's benefit, the two of them always together. Dinner was in the refrigerator, which Richie heated up on the stove and shared with the dog. The boy liked being around the animal, caring for his newfound friend. What he failed to realize was that the dog was also caring for him.

CHAPTER 8

THE DOG RAISED an eyebrow at the distant sound of a vehicle accelerating from the four corners. It was well after midnight, and while sleep had overwhelmed the boy more than an hour earlier, the dog seemed to understand that there was someone absent. The vehicle did not dispense the rattles and squeals of Becka Small's car, but as it slowed and turned into the driveway, the dog snapped its head up, ears pricked upward in anticipation. With the slamming of a car door and then another, the dog's attention was out through the wall and toward the voices of people in the front yard. With the creaking on the steps leading up to the wooden porch, the dog stood, looked back at the sleeping boy, effortlessly bound to the floor alongside the bed, and moved to the slit formed by the almost closed door.

The voices grew louder. There was the voice that the dog knew to be that of the woman, the woman that had lived with the boy, the voice from inside the walls that the dog had heard while huddled under the steps of the porch for the last several nights. There was a second voice, a harsh voice, a loud voice, a deep voice that seemed to grow louder, even though it was no closer. And the dog recognized it as the voice of a man. The dog looked back at the boy as he rolled over, partially awakened by the noise on the porch.

The boy patted the bed where the dog had lain and sleepily called out to her, "Lady. Come here, Lady."

For the first time in their day, the dog ignored the boy and turned away to listen to the voices as if suspicious of what was happening. There was the creak in the boards on the porch and then the crackle of the poorly fitted exterior door as it opened, and the voices became clear.

Richie turned over and tried to defeat the feeling of a deep sleep that clung in his head. He sat up, tried to bring moisture to his mouth, and instinctively searched for his glasses on the nightstand next to his bed.

"Well, how about a drink then?" The voice was that of a man who slurred his words.

"I told you I don't have anything but milk and water, and anyway, I think you have had quite enough," Becka replied.

"Hey, I drove you all the way out here. Don't you think I deserve—"

Becka's comment cut him off. "Really, I do appreciate the ride. That junker of mine surely picked a good night to conk out."

"Just the battery," the man responded. "If someone only had a set of jumper cables, but since I'm all the way out here, there isn't any reason you can't be a little more friendly."

"Oh, I think there is plenty of reason." Becka tried to make the comment quite clear but with a quipish tone of voice.

Richie positioned the glasses on his nose, wrapped the ends of the frame over his ears, and climbed out of his bed.

"Now that's not a very nice thing to say!" The man's voice deepened with a gruffness being added to it. "I might just be getting the impression you don't like me, and that would be, well, that just wouldn't be right now, would it?"

"Just go, will you!" She spoke these words in total sincerity and with the sound of the door creaking as if being closed. "I think you have the wrong impression."

"I don't think so, little lady!" There was the sound of shuffling feet in the doorway, the thunderous bang of the door being thrown open against the wall of the trailer, and the hideous sound of someone being slapped.

"Get out of here!" Becka screamed.

"Hit me, will you!" The man's surly voice sounded mean. "I'll show you!"

What happened next was a blur to Richie. There was a scream, the light from the living room streaming into the bedroom as the dog forced the door open with her body, and the sickening thud of someone being slapped or hit. He reached the now open door just as the man, his back turned toward the bedroom and one hand holding on to Becka, raised his arm to hit his mother again. As he swung his arm down, the dog somehow bounded over the couch, momentarily up onto the man's back, and then clamped her jaws onto the still raised arm. Becka Small half-twisted free and stumbled away from the man over the table in the middle of the room and onto the sofa as the momentum and power of the dog dragged the man headlong into the television stand.

The dog was in frenzy. At first, she remained locked on the extended arm, tearing through the jacket and shirt and then into the skin of the forearm with a vicious shaking of her head. The man screamed out, but it was barely audible over the deep long vicious growls of the animal. The man tried to reposition himself in order to kick out at the animal. The dog reacted. She avoided the kick, momentarily let go, avoided a second kick, and then latched onto the arm again when the man tried to backhand the dog away. The fur on her back bristled upward, and with extraordinary power, she pulled on the man's outstretched arm and extended it back and then over his head, dragging the man away from the couch. Blood began to build up in the man's torn jacket and shirt, and he lay there helpless, the dog clenching his extended arm securely in her jaws. If he moved, the dog tore into the arm with another vicious shake of her head.

"Call off your dog!" Even the man's plea caused the dog to pull on the arm.

Becka lay on the coach, dazed by the blow to the side of her head and then by what was happening in front of her. It was Richie who took control.

"Lady!" He spoke the name sternly. "Come here!"

The dog immediately let go of the man's arm, gingerly backed away, and positioned herself strategically on Richie's left and next to the couch. Richie moved over toward the couch, the dog now standing in front of both of them, separating them from the man.

"You had better get out of here!" Richie commanded.

The man rolled onto his back, a smirk coming to his face as he looked at the boy one-quarter his size. The expression did not go unnoticed, and the dog responded by crouching, baring her teeth, and snapping out at one of the man's legs. Suddenly, he must have recognized that blood was gathering in the shredded fabric of his shirt and jacket with the onset of what would have been terrible pain. His eyes glazed as he pulled back his leg and cowered up against the wall.

"Mister!" Richie commanded. "You get out of here, or I'll let her loose on you again."

"Okay, okay!" The man gulped for air, got to his knees, and stumbled out the doorway toward the car in the driveway.

As Richie heard the vehicle's engine start and the gravel flail up against the wall of the trailer from its spinning wheels, he went to the door, slammed it shut, and twisted the deadbolt lock shut.

Richie turned to his mother as she tried to raise herself into a sitting position. Blood trickled from a jagged cut on her cheekbone and under the swelling welt along the side of her head and next to her eye. He helped her into a seated position and realized that ice would help stop both the bleeding and the swelling. Dragging a chair into the kitchen, he opened the top of the refrigerator, hopped up onto the chair, and took out the two trays of ice. Then he placed most of the cubes into a clean dish towel and cinched the four corners into a tight knot.

"Here, Mom."

He handed her the ice pack and watched as she gingerly placed it on the large lump that was forming next to her eye. The swelling seemed to slow the bleeding, but blood had gathered on her hand and arm, on the sleeve of her blouse, and on one of the pillows of the couch. He went back to the kitchen and ran a clean towel under the faucet and rung out the cold water. Using the dampened cloth, he wiped the blood from her cheek and then her hand and arm.

"I'm going to run down and get Jennie," Richie said.

"No, I'll be okay." His mother was starting to sound more coherent. "And anyway, she and the rest of the family are visiting Charlie over in Big Rapids."

She took a deep breath, examined the rest of the room, and leaned her head back along the shoulder of the couch.

"Well, we managed to crush a table." Her gaze was toward the splintered remains of what once had been a low table positioned in front of the couch. "At least, the television stand didn't collapse."

Richie looked into the corner of the room where the television teetered while still sitting on it stand but precariously balanced against the wall where the stand had come to rest.

"And this?" His mother's hand was being softly nudged by the snout of the dog.

"A dog," Richie said sheepishly.

"I know that, young man." His mother turned her head and winced from pain.

"Maybe I should run into town. Get someone to take you to the hospital."

"I'll be fine." She shook her head as if clearing out the cobwebs and managed a smile. "I was asking about our new guest."

"Her name is Lady. She is a good dog too. Really gentle."

His mother managed a half laugh through the pain. "Did you say gentle? Well, if that was gentle, I sure wouldn't want to make her mad."

"I mean until now." Richie recognized how lame his statement had sounded.

"Where did she come from?" Becka asked.

Richie shrugged his shoulders. "But can we keep her?"

"Well, she must belong to someone, and when we find out—"

Richie interrupted. "But until we do, that is if we do, can she stay here?"

"I guess."

Richie went to the kitchen for more ice and another clean towel. And as he did, Becka tapped the dog on her head. Softly, she spoke the words. "Thank you, Lady."

The dog nudged harder up against Becka's hand, turned her own head, and focused the dark eyes in her direction as if realizing that she was accepted by not only the boy but now also his mother.

CHAPTER 9

THE DARK BLUE vehicle with the markings of the Michigan State Police did not pass by but instead turned into the driveway in front of the old trailer. Richie had just walked the dog down to the four corners and back, and they turned to face the occupant that was exiting the cruiser. The expression on the face of both the boy and dog seemed to reveal that what was happening was not that unexpected.

"Good morning, young man." The voice was slow and meticulous as if assuring anyone spoken to that the words were clear and distinct.

The boy and dog just looked back at the man dressed in the dark blue uniform and placing his hat on his head as he stepped away from the vehicle.

"Is this the Small residence?"

"Yes, sir," Richie responded reluctantly.

"That your dog, young man?" the officer inquired.

"Yes, sir."

"Is she friendly?"

Richie peered at the man, knowing that what happened last night was the reason for the visit. "Yes, sir, she is very friendly." His statement was a clear pronouncement.

"Is your mother or father home?" he asked.

"My mother is inside, but she is still in bed."

Ten thirty on Saturday morning and the mother was still in bed, the police officer thought, probably a party that had gotten out of hand. He had no sympathy for people who ignored their children, especially on the weekend when they should be home together. But Frank Savage had called in the complaint about being bitten by a yellow dog, and the doctor had told the officer that he had the bites to prove it.

"Young man, it is important that I speak with her. Could you get her up?"

"Yes, sir." Richie pondered the idea of leaving the policeman standing outside. Then he thought it only hospitable to invite him in, maybe earning some credits for the questions that were surely going to follow. He held the door open as the officer approached the porch. "Sir, come in while I get her."

The officer stepped into the trailer, and Richie motioned him toward the couch. The man decided to stand, and Richie entered his mother's bedroom and closed the door. Seeming to sense that a problem accompanied the uniform, the dog set herself down on her haunches in front of the bedroom door and concentrated her eyes on the man, adding a sense of curiosity by raising her ears.

The officer looked around the room and into the kitchen. The trailer was old but well kept. Except for a table turned over on its top, everything seemed to be in place. He noticed the super glue on a piece of newspaper next to the table and realized someone was trying to fasten two of the legs back to the table.

As he swiveled to get a look in the kitchen, he was surprised by the feel of the soft fur of the dog's head being brushed against the knuckles of the hand holding his hat. He looked down at the dog. She had silently crossed the room and repositioned herself on her haunches, her tail waggling from side to side over the old carpeting. He sat down and sank into the old sofa behind him, the dog having strategically positioned herself at his knee. Almost instinctively, he reached out and petted the dog on the top of the head and back around the ears. She seemed gentle enough, not the vicious attack dog that was described in the report that had been faxed over to his desk from the city constable that morning.

He noted that someone had attempted to rub out a recent stain on the cushion next to him, both the cushion and armrest appearing to still be damp. Another damp spot could also be seen on the carpeting next to the overturned table. Something drew his attention to the small table and lamp that sat behind the sofa, and he stood to examine what he had noticed. Small flecks of dried blood were on the base of the lamp and on the table. So, he concluded, there had been a fight or something in the trailer and recently. He looked down at the dog next to him. The dog brushed up against the side of his uniform pants, demanding more attention. It was then that the bedroom door opened.

A small woman in her late twenties and bundled in a thick robe entered the room. She stumbled slightly, and at first, he thought she still might be recovering from whatever they used in partying the night before.

"Yes, sir. Can I help you?" Her speech was slurred, and she barely moved her mouth, her mannerism seemingly confirming his suspicions.

"Ma'am, Sergeant Learner with the Michigan State Police. We have a report of a. . ." He had positioned himself to see her, but even though she tried to tilt her face away from him, what he saw hung his statement out in midair. He noticed how the boy helped his mother stand and held a cold compress in his free hand.

Sergeant Learner's mannerism immediately changed. His voice softened, but his question was direct. "How many times did Frank Savage hit you?"

She turned and peered back at him. A grotesque bulge disfigured her pretty round face. "Sir, I don't want any trouble. We are new here, and it's tough enough on my boy. We surely don't want to make any trouble."

The officer moved toward her to help while motioning toward the sofa. And as he did, he noted how the dog positioned herself at the woman's side, always vigilant as to the man's intentions. He sat down in the chair next to the sofa while she attempted to make herself comfortable.

"Son, can you freshen that ice pack?" he asked.

The term *son* surprised him. Why would he call him son? Richie thought as he picked up the pack and went to the kitchen.

"Ms. Small, the first thing we have to do is have that looked at." He pointed to the side of her face. "There is a walk-in emergency care center in Mancelona. You can have it checked there."

"I'll be fine." She protested. "A day or two and I'll be back at work." Work, she thought, she hadn't told anyone that she would not be in that afternoon, and then she wondered how she could afford the cost of a doctor's visit.

"It is something that I will have to insist upon," he responded as he almost picked her mind clean of what she was thinking. "If it is a matter of money, we will be taking care of that. So I want you to tell me what happened."

She protested again and then fell silent. It was Richie who spoke up.

"Sir, my mother's car broke down at the restaurant where she works. And this man, the man that was here last night, gave her a ride home."

"Richie, that's enough," Becka stated firmly.

"No, Mom, no man pushes himself into our home and hits you like that for no reason and gets away with it." He stared at his mother, knowing that he seldom spoke over her command. "If it wasn't for Lady, he would have hit you again."

"Is that when the dog attacked Mr. Savage?" the officer asked.

"I don't know his name," Richie responded.

"It was Frank." His mother began to speak sheepishly. "Look, he is a regular at the restaurant out at the expressway. I thought I could trust him for a ride. Maybe he had a little too much to drink before he came in. I'm sure he didn't mean for anything to happen."

Learner appeared disgusted with her explanation. "Ms. Small, no man has the right to lay a hand on a woman." He then changed the subject. "Would you go back into the bedroom and get dressed? That cut is going to need a stitch or two, and you may not have noticed it, but there is some bleeding in the eye."

He looked toward Richie and used that strange term to address him. "I'll be honest with you, son. I will have to have that dog looked at, even though she was only protecting your mother. So why don't you and I take your mother over to Mancelona and then stop in and see Dr. Wild. He can look Lady over and give her a clean bill of health."

Learner, Sergeant Learner, not a common name, Richie thought. Maybe he was his teacher's brother. Then Richie saw the gold band on the officer's left hand and thought otherwise. He was nice, nice like Mrs. Learner, Richie thought, maybe he was her husband. But he let the matter lay as he got ready to go.

CHAPTER 10

AFTER DROPPING OFF Becka Small at the hospital in Mancelona, Sergeant Learner asked Richie to accompany him. After parking in front of an appliance store, they left the dog in the police cruiser and went inside, Richie being told to stand at the front door. If the man whom Sergeant Learner spoke to was the man at the trailer the previous night, Richie was to indicate so by simply nodding his head yes. Richie did as he was told and stood at the door while the officer waited for a customer to leave and then spoke to the man behind the counter.

"Mr. Savage." The officer set a notebook on the counter. "I'm Sergeant Learner with the Michigan State Police." He momentarily turned toward Richie as he spoke, and Richie nodded yes.

"You reported a dog attack last night." Learner's voice was very calm and low, almost inaudible to Richie.

"That animal tore into my arm." The man spoke vehemently. "Vicious thing that ought to be destroyed!" He held up a heavily bandaged hand and arm as evidence. "No, I'm going to see to it that it is destroyed!"

Learner opened the pad of paper and withdrew a pen from his breast pocket. "Let me get the details, Mr. Savage. Where did this happen?"

"Out past Townline and I think it was on Swaffer, Rebecca Small's place." The man peered over the officer's shoulder, trying to get a look at the person who remained standing in the door. "Gave the girl a ride home. Opened the door for her and was on the way back to my car when this dog attacks me."

Richie immediately responded, "That's a lie. He pushed his way in and—"

"That will be enough, Richard." Learner's firm comment cut him off.

"How many drinks you have last night, Frank? Four, five, maybe more?"

"A couple." The man swallowed hard several times, his Adam's apple seeming to bulge with each gulp while the officer remained silent. "Maybe four or five but not more," he finally responded.

Learner glared at him for several long moments before he spoke. "Now, Frank, I want you to think about this before you answer because if you lie to me, it is just one more thing that just might not be in your best interest. Did you hit her just the one time or more than once?"

"Hit her? Me hit her, hit, hit, a woman?" The man attempted to be firm, but his voice cracked. "I would never hit. . ."

"Mr. Savage, you had better—" Learner's voice was deep and determined.

"Just once, once. . .that's all, just once." The man peered straight at the officer. "Only once. The dog jumped on me after that." The man's Adam's apple bounced around in his throat as if on a rubber band.

"In the house?" Learner asked.

"It was a trailer," Savage responded.

"It was her home!" Learner spoke the words slowly and with conviction and then remained silent for a long moment, allowing what he had said sink in.

"What I have in front of me is a man, what about six feet two, drunk, who is inside a woman's house, is told to leave, and hits her. A woman about five feet three inches tall, maybe one-hundred and five pounds tops. Hits her so hard that he puts her in the hospital."

"Hospital!" the man responded.

Learner seemed to ignore the response. "Then he files a false police report about a dog attack." He peered directly at the man as he spoke. "He tries to lie to the investigating officer." The officer stopped. "Were you that intoxicated,

Mr. Savage, that you don't even know you many times you struck Ms. Small?"

"It was only once. I didn't think I hit her that hard, but it was just once."

The police officer remained silent for several moments, while Frank Savage stood motionless, motionless except for the sweat profusely running down his forehead.

"Here is what I am going to do." Learner closed the notebook. "Since she has no insurance, I'm going to have a hospital bill sent over to you for Ms. Small, which you are going to pay. Then I am going to have a vet bill sent over to you for the dog, her shots, a checkup, and maybe a year's supply of dog food. Then I am going to check where Ms. Small works and find out how much she makes. You will gladly pay for the wages due her, and then I am going to have her car repaired and send you the bill, or. . ." He left the statement hanging in midair.

"Or what?" Savage questioned meekly.

"Or I will arrest you for home invasion, assault, and battery of a woman half your size, filing a false police report and then obstructing an investigation by lying to me." Learner paused.

Savage had turned a chalky white, the perspiration gathering in dark blotches in the collar of his light blue shirt and under his arms. He momentarily wavered, and Richie thought he might pass out or, at least, chuck up his breakfast. Finally, he gulped some air, bounced his Adam's apple from the top of his chest to just under his chin, and responded, "Send me the bills."

"I thought you'd see it my way." Learner turned and took a couple steps away from the counter and then swiveled back toward the man.

"How long for that hand and arm to heal?" Learner asked.

"Six weeks," Savage answered meekly.

There was a rumble in the sergeant's voice, deep and low and laced with a tone that made even Richie shutter, leaving no doubt that he meant what he said. "Mr. Savage, how about in a couple of months I come back here and you try to hit me like you did Ms. Small? You take the first shot. Pick your best and try picking on someone other than a woman. What do you say?"

Frank Savage blinked, the sweat running profusely down his face, the front of his shirt now also a deep color of blue, and a trembling started in his body.

"Come on, Frank, whatcha say? No uniform, just man to man."

Savage could barely stand, and a chattering of his teeth now accompanied his trembling.

It was then that Richie noticed something. Learner was wide, real wide. The width of his shoulders stretched the dark blue of the uniform across his back, flattening it against muscle that rippled when he moved his arms or turned his head. His shoulders did not slope down from his neck but ran rigid to the top of each arm, a pronounced bulge visible under the material of his shirt near each shoulder. His chest was just as broad, filling his uniform and stretching across his body when he took a deep breath. His stomach was flat, almost indented, and his upper body just sloped into the belt around his trousers. His arms were thick and muscular, bulging as he flexed his arms, even the forearms broadening as they left his wrist into oblong masses of muscle. The collar of his shirt closed tightly around his thick neck, but as he turned, his neck muscles pulled at the fabric and rippled down over his shoulders and onto his back. He was maybe a full six inches shorter than Frank Savage. Yeah, Sergeant Learner was short, real short, but by no means, by no one's definition, was he small. The word *small* was the least appropriate manner to describe him. In fact, he was just the opposite. He was massive.

CHAPTER 11

"IS THERE A student by the name of Richard Small in the fifth grade?" Bob Learner asked his wife from across the other side of the bed.

She turned from her book and peered over the top of her reading glasses. "Richard Small, sure, and he is in my room. Why do you ask?" A look of concern suddenly crossed her face. "He hasn't been hurt, has he?"

"Oh no, he's fine," he responded. "But someone got a little rough with his mother the other night." He anticipated her next question. "And she is fine too, a little bruised up, but she'll be fine."

"Did you find out what happened?" The look on her face displayed worry.

"That's taken care of, but what about Richard?" he asked.

She seemed relieved by her husband's answer and refocused on his question. "Well, he's a nice boy. Well behaved, good manners, never misses school." She thought about it for a moment. "No, he was absent yesterday, Friday. Principal Glum tried to call, but they don't have a telephone number for the Smalls."

"They don't have a telephone," Carol Learner's husband of six years responded as he turned on his side in their spacious bed. "The boy and his mother live in a modular out on Swaffer."

"I thought those were all nice homes out that way. Remember we looked at that big colonial on the hill."

"The other side of Townline, farther to the west." He too recalled the house they had thought about purchasing before deciding it was too expensive and settling on an older Victorian-style home in the village. "I think she said it was owned by a grandparent."

"And the father?" She noticed how he had failed to mention one.

"Killed in Kuwait about ten years ago. From what I got from Ms. Small, I think he wasn't even aware that he was going to be a father."

She laid the book down on her chest. "Oh, how sad." There was a questioning in her voice accompanied with an obvious concern. "Maybe that's part of Richard's problem. He's strangely aloof from the other members of the class. Smaller than all of them, new to the community, and, from what you say, no father figure and not real well off."

Bob knew he had to continue the conversation because his wife would fall into worry while now contemplating how she could help the boy. "They have a pet dog, a Labrador Retriever."

"That's funny," she answered momentarily, stowing her thoughts. "We talked about pets in class about two weeks ago, and I remember that everyone had a pet of some type—dogs, cats, hamsters, gold fish—everyone except Richard Small."

Her statement confirmed his suspicions. "I have the feeling that she was a stray. They never really answered how long they had the dog. But I will tell you one thing, that dog and that boy are really close, like she has been with him for years. Nobody, and I mean absolutely nobody, will ever get between that dog and that boy or for that matter the mother either."

Sergeant Learner went on and told her about the incident involving Frank Savage, knowing that she would not reveal police matters to anyone else. He also realized that his wife would now be diligently searching for ways to help both the boy and the mother.

"What do you think of the idea in getting him involved with the football team and the weight club?"

She smiled at him. "I thought you were going to say that."

"And why do you say that?" he inquired.

"Maybe its six years of marriage. I'm starting to be able to read your mind." She reached over the bed and playfully poked him in the ribs. "Means that you can't keep any secrets from me."

"Well, I was just thinking—"

She interrupted him. "I know what you were thinking, and I'll tell you. He reminds you of someone. . ." She focused her gaze on her husband as she removed the reading glasses and placed them on the nightstand next to the bed. "And that person is you. What did they tell you in high school, that you were too small to play?"

"Yeah, and so. . ."

"And so when we get set up on a blind date at Michigan State, I'm going out with this All-American linebacker whom no one mentions, no one even considers as being too small to play."

"Well, five feet eight inches isn't big," he countered.

"No, five feet eight inches and two hundred thirty pounds, able to bench-press four hundred pounds."

"Four hundred and forty." He corrected her.

Her smile broadened. "See, he does, he reminds you of you."

"I was just thinking that without a father figure, having an adult male around would be good for him."

"Sure it would." She slipped over to his side of the bed and playfully hugged him. "But before I allow it, I want you to admit it, just admit it."

His wife was not that much shorter than he, but when he wrapped his massive arms around her and drew her up into his broad chest, she all but disappeared. "You're right," he said with a sense of reflection in his voice. "He does remind me of someone."

She liked being hugged by her husband, and it was a long moment before she responded. She turned her head and looked straight into the face she loved. "It would be good for the both of you." And then she kissed him softly on the lips and then kissed him again this time with the passion that continued to grow between them, that night and in every night to follow.

CHAPTER 12

THE EUREKA SPRINGS football team had become a legend in the eight short years that Jeff Ball had been head coach. In those eight seasons, they had won the last seven league championships, even though the school had the smallest enrollment in the ten-team league. Seven trips to Michigan's playoffs had resulted in five trips to the semifinals and two to the state finals where they lost to Kalamazoo Catholic Central each time, the state's perennial class C champion.

While Jeff Ball was the head coach, everyone in the community recognized that Assistant Head Coach Bob Learner was just as instrumental for the team's success. It was Coach Learner who had created the Eureka Springs Panthers Weight Training and Conditioning Club. And while Eureka Springs typically had between twenty and twenty-five players on their sideline compared to the fifty or sixty across the field, it was the Panthers who were the ones that typically prevailed. They prevailed because they were stronger and in better condition than their opponents. It was anticipated that when you played the Panthers, you were going to face the hardest hitting team in the league and players that never seemed to run out of energy. It was Coach Learner and his off-season weight training and conditioning program that created that advantage.

To be chosen the middle school student assistant for the club was an honor that every middle school boy sought. Typically, it would go to one of the seventh- or eighth-grade football players. It would entail working the remainder of the school year and the following summer with the club and then through the next year's football season. It usually brought recognition and notoriety to a middle school player who would probably be a future Panther team member, if not a star player. For Richie Small, a fifth grader, to be chosen seemed to be a big mistake, a decision that had absolutely no rhyme or reason whatsoever. No one really believed it when the notice was placed on the board outside Assistant Principal R. U. Bad's office. One of the seventh-grade boys even ripped it off the board, thinking it was a joke perpetrated by someone with no sense of humor. But Richie was starting to think it wasn't.

After receiving the written invitation detailing the obligations and tradition of such a choice by Coach Learner, his mother had to be convinced by Mrs. Learner. She had initially refused. It was during an after-school conference, while relegated to the hallway, that Richie overheard Mrs. Learner say how much she enjoyed Richie and that it would be good for him. Then she said how much she and her husband desired to someday have a son as nice as him, and it was then that his mother acquiesced. It was also at that time that Richie realized just how much he respected his teacher.

Still, no one in the middle school believed it, and Richie almost didn't either as he stood on the porch of their trailer in late November. The Panthers had just finished their season, another heartbreaking loss to Kalamazoo Central in the state finals. It was time to start training for next season, and now he was standing on the porch waiting for one of the football players to pick him up at five thirty in the afternoon, as instructed, for the first scheduled off season workout. The only problem was that it was five o'clock.

Lady was sitting at his side looking out at the street as if also waiting in anticipation. Eventually, after spending thirty minutes in the cold, a car came from out in the country, slowed, and turned into the driveway. Richie immediately ordered Lady back into the house, pulled the door shut behind her, and bounded out toward the vehicle even before it came to a complete stop. The right side rear door opened, and a person shaped like a block of granite and wearing the blue-and-yellow varsity jacket of the Eureka Springs Panthers stepped from the car. Richie took it as the obvious sign as to how he was getting in and slid into the middle of the back seat and next to another blue-and-yellow jacket.

"Richard Small." The driver turned and looked over the seat as he backed out of the driveway. "I'm Carl Leader," he said.

"Just call him Captain," the other player in the back seat chimed in. "Still think he rigged the election." There seemed to be a joking attitude in the comment.

"Yeah, right." Leader smiled and then nodded to the player in the back seat. "That's Sam Fingers. We call him Slant because he runs a great slant pattern. Just wish he had a better set of hands."

Slant reached out and pushed on the captain's shoulder. "Just hit me with a spiral, not those lame ducks you throw."

As Richie forced a smile, he found a gigantic hand reaching out toward him from the player who had opened the door.

"Ben Shoulders, everyone calls me Big Ben." The voice was so deep that it seemed to rumble off of Richie's rib cage as if his chest was one big drum and then radiate up through his neck and add additional volume to what he was hearing.

Richie reached out to shake Big Ben's hand and watched as his entire forearm disappeared inside the grasp, hoping that his hand was not going to be simply crushed flat like a postage stamp.

"Hey, bro, Tyrone Walker."

Richie looked up into the broad white smile of what appeared to be a mouthful of extra teeth. The player in the front passenger seat was black, black like wet coal, and the wide smile just accented the darkness of his complexion. His clear wide eyes examined Richie over a pair of sunglasses that he wore more on the tip of his nose than over his eyes. Finally, the player extended his hand, but his fist was closed. Instinctively, Richie put his fist out, not knowing what to expect, and was surprised when Walker bumped his closed fist against his and then hammered down on his still closed hand.

"They call me Speed. And you don't have to ask why."

The others in the car chuckled as they finished backing out the driveway and turned to head into Eureka Springs.

"Hey, my man," Speed said from the front seat. "What we be calling you? Richard just ain't gonna be cutting it."

Richie looked around at the four varsity jacket-clad players, not knowing what to say. Even if he could get the lump from his throat, he realized he was too overwhelmed to utter any type of meaningful sounds. He just hoped that the rumbling in his stomach would not result in a reexamination of his recent snack.

"Come on, my man. What are we gonna be calling you? You just gotta have a nickname." Walker demanded.

Richie swallowed hard, felt saliva come from somewhere in his mouth, moistened his lips, and then with all his strength, he mustered a response. "My mother calls me Richie."

For some reason, the two boys in the back seat chuckled.

"Richie, come on now. That ain't making it. You need a nickname, a handle, something we can call you," Speed continued.

"Richie, like Richie Rich, the comic strip character," Big Ben said, his deep voice pounding Richie down in his seat.

"No, man, this man isn't any comic strip character. He's the new student assistant for the club. He needs proper credentials," Speed said.

"Yeah, man," Slant commented. "The boy needs a nickname." He reached over and rubbed his hand through Richie's hair. "This Richie stuff, well, that's for kids. We are going to be turning this boy into a man." Slant chuckled.

Their voices displayed a sense of urgency that made Richie think that nothing good was going to come out of the conversation.

"Leave the boy be." Carl Leader's voice was direct and sure. "He will come up with something when he wants to."

"Yes, sir." Richie gulped his reply.

"It's Carl, Carl or Captain. There is no need to be calling me sir," Leader said sternly. "Coach Ball and Coach Learner, you call them sir." He looked at Richie through the rearview mirror as he spoke. "But I guess we had better come up with something before these other three goofballs hang something on you that might not be that appropriate. They've done it before." Everyone in the car chuckled at the statement, everyone except Richie.

"Okay, Captain, what do you suggest?" Slant commented. "And who you calling a goofball?"

Leader ignored the question. "What's your middle name?"

Richie looked back at the captain through the mirror. "James, sir." He tried to stop the second of the two words he had spoken as previously instructed, but it just spilled out over his lips.

"Richie Jimmie." Slant snorted out the names. "That doesn't do anything for me."

Speed turned and looked over the back seat. There was a certain understanding in his eyes, an understanding that Richie recognized. And while Ben and Slant talked about some girl in their American History class named Casey, Tyrone Walker continued examining the young boy in the back seat.

Captain pulled into the parking lot that separated the high school and elementary school and parked up near the front of the building where several groups of students were waiting to take the late bus home. Ben and Slant flung open the rear doors and were immediately out of the car, slamming the doors behind them. Carl started to open his door, but Walker's tug on the sleeve of his varsity jacket reseated him behind the wheel.

"How about RJ? What do you think?" The slang in his speech had disappeared, and Walker looked first at Richie and then back at the captain.

"Well, what do you think Mr. Small?" Carl asked.

Richie simply nodded yes.

"Settled then. RJ it is!" Walker's voice exhibited a positive attitude as he turned back and opened the front door. "Let's get a cracking, RJ."

"Come on, RJ," Carl said while tilting his head in the direction of the high school gym. "I'll show you around."

Richie reopened the door and stepped in behind the two varsity jacket-clad players as they walked toward the gym. A group of middle school students waiting to take one of the late buses home gawked at the growing group of football players approaching from the several cars parked in the lot. Richie remained oblivious to what was going on and just attempted to keep up and not embarrass himself by making a wrong turn. As they approached the group of middle school students, several pointed at Richie.

"Hey, it's true! Smallie is the student assistant for the club!" He heard a seventh-grade boy that he recognized utter the comment with a sense of disbelief.

"Can't be!" he heard another exclaim.

For some reason, Richie tucked his head down and tried to avoid eye contact with the group of students, and that might have been his fatal mistake. For in the sea of sixth, seventh, and eighth graders was Clarence Goodfellow. He had served a detention over some miscue that he somehow failed to explain away. The innocence that he was able to spread across his wide freckled face and through his gigantic grin had not convinced the appropriate authority that it was all someone else's fault.

As Richie approached, Clarence positioned himself and loaded up his right arm. For he was going to place one of the most devastating slug-ohs of all time on the tip of shoulder of the unsuspecting Richie Small. It would be a lethal one, the recipient unable to anticipate the knuckle crackling blow to the very tip of the shoulder. It would surely bring tears to his eyes. It would wilt the arm into a hanging mass of Jell-O, fingers uselessly tingling at the end of an arm. If administered properly, shooting pains would race up and down the arm and maybe into the side of his neck. Then there would be a deadness that would last for several long minutes, making the victim, while in panic, wonder if he would ever be able to raise his arm again.

Maybe they would have to amputate. They wouldn't, but it would be sore for the better part of a week. Most importantly, if delivered properly, there would be no bruise left as evidence.

And what better place, Clarence thought, to continue his revenge on Richie Small but in front of soon-to-be admiring middle schoolers. He was surrounded by his peers and with not a teacher or principal in sight. He would be able to grin from ear to ear while watching his victim wither in pain, accepting the accolades of his fellow schoolmates without having to worry about being caught. It would be perfection.

As Richie continued in his direction, he would soon perfectly position the very tip of his shoulder at the most desirable location of all time. Clarence pulled his arm back, back even further than normal in anticipation of administering the blow until even his skin stretched itself firmly across the blubber on his chest. He stretched back so far that his pants, already too tight around his walrus-sized waist, started to cut off the circulation going down to the bottom half of his body, bringing a slight numbness to his feet. For a moment, he thought the button clasping the front of his pants might jettison itself like a rocket from under the fat lapping over his belt and eventually end up in orbit somewhere out in space, if, at least, not across the parking lot. As Richie approached, he waited and tried to suck in his stomach in order to avoid the launch of the button. And then he was there, in the perfect position, and Clarence let fly with the master, the crème de la crème, the ultimate, the biggest, the best, and the most devastating slug-oh of all, aimed right at the very tip of Richie's shoulder.

Richie never saw it coming. What he did see was the large black hand of someone in front of him sweep back and just graze his shoulder, stopping between the tip of his shoulder and a fat freckled fist that was now engulfed in its grip. It must have been like hitting a brick wall. The arm to which the fist was attached seemed to set up a vibration that rattled back up the arm, over the shoulder, through the neck, and into the head. It was as if the very eyes of Clarence Goodfellow now seemingly bounced up and down in his big round head like they were being dribbled on a basketball floor.

"Ow!" Clarence bellowed loudly, the black fist having closed around his hand.

"Hey!" Walker said sternly. "What you be doing to my man RJ here!"

Clarence seemed oblivious to the statement as he tried to simultaneously withdraw his hand from the grip and stop the chatter that had worked its way into his teeth.

Walker released his hold on Clarence's hand while perspiration started to bead up on the fat boy's face and run down and around cheeks that looked chalkier than normal. Goodfellow shook his fist as if it were on fire, doing a little dance while standing in place; the motion started a mini-eruption of giggling fat over his entire body. Panting sounds emanated from his mouth as he tried to stop the stinging that started in his fist and ran directly to his brain.

"Come on, RJ," Walker stated while placing his hand on Richie's shoulder. "Porky there seems to be at a loss for words."

The other middle school students laughed and pointed at Clarence as the pain subsided, and he slowed his little dance to just a slight trembling of fat.

"Oink, oink," one eighth grader bellowed in Clarence's direction.

"Here, piggy," another hollered as if calling pigs to supper.

As he turned into the high school, Richie looked back. In the group of middle school students, all pointing in his direction, stood Clarence Goodfellow, still shaking his arm. He deserved it, deserved being made to look the fool, but for some strange reason, Richie felt sorry, sorry for someone who was being pointed at and laughed at by his fellow classmates. That's right, he felt sorry for Clarence Goodfellow, and he really could not understand why.

CHAPTER 13

"HEY, RJ," A big burly offensive lineman by the name of Bret called out. "I need a couple of forty-fives over here and a spot."

It was becoming less of a struggle to lift up the forty-five-pound circular weight and carry it over to the bench, but Richie's body didn't seem to notice it. It had been two full weeks and eight sessions in the weight room, during which Richie had acted as the middle school assistant. He helped with the large circular weights for the bars, refilled the chalk boxes that the players used to dry their hands, picked up towels, recorded total pounds lifted and number of repetitions for some of the players in their daily workout journals, and spotted for some of the lifters.

Spotting or being a spotter was his favorite. It meant that he would stand over the bar that suspended weights that might be three or four times his own body weight. If the lifter needed that little extra help in completing his final lifts, it would be Richie who would reach over, grasp the bar, and, with a steady pull, offer enough assistance to replace the bar safely back in the rack.

He staggered and swayed as he carried one of the forty-five-pound disks over to the bench press. The disk was half his body weight, and he huffed and puffed while trying to make it appear that he was not straining every muscle in his body to simply get the weight from the rack to the bar. It reality, he had to use every muscle just to keep from having the weight pull him straight to the floor or, worse yet, have him fall backward, the big round circular plate, he thought, probably capable of crushing him like a bug. And then as he approached the bar, he took aim at the thick steel end and tried to run the bar through the hole in the middle of the weight as if threading a needle but with something infinitely heavier. He hoped not to miss thinking that if he did, his forward momentum would probably take him right through the far wall and out on to the school parking lot. Luckily, his first attempt was right on, and he slid the plate up against two that were already in position on that side of the bar and tried to catch his breath. It was now three forty-five-pound disks on each side of the bar and the thirty-five-pound bar, a total of 305 pounds.

"Spot me, will you?" Bret said as he positioned himself on the bench. "I'm going to try for five."

Richie stood on the platform at the head of the bench and counted out each lift or repetition, rep for short, and poised his hands around the bar. After the lifter struggled ever so slightly on the fourth, he grasped the bar and, with a steady tug, led the bar back up and into the rack on the fifth rep.

Bret sat up and rotated his shoulders in order to clear the slight numbness that accompanied lifting such weight. He looked over at Richie. "What do you want on the bar, RJ?"

The question puzzled Richie, and he peered back at Bret with an inquisitive look on his face.

"What? It's been a week now, right?" Bret took off the forty-five-pound disks, one in each hand, walked over the storage rack, and started replacing them on the spindle. "Coach says that after a week, that is if you lasted a week, you're part of the club." He turned back toward him. "And that means you work out just like the rest of us."

The puzzled look remained on Richie's face.

"Okay then. Since it seems you swallowed your tongue, how about we start off with a couple of ten-pound plates?"

Bret slid a ten-pound weight on each end. With the thirty-five-pound bar, Richie faced the challenge of bench-pressing over one-half of his body weight. Upon Bret's continuing insistence, he reluctantly positioned himself back down on the bench, his forehead under the bar, and grasped it firmly with both hands. With great anticipation represented by a breath so deep that he thought his chest would explode, he lifted up and outward on the bar.

"One, two, three. Come on, my man, let's get it on for a total of ten." Tyrone Walker's voice came from somewhere behind him and over his head as he counted out the reps. "Breathe out, my man. No sense wasting all that effort on simply holding your breath, nine and ten." Walker finished the count and had his hands near the bar as Richie guided it back safely into the rack without assistance.

He sat up, like the high school lifters did, and wondered if he was experiencing the "burn," as they called it, when the muscle group used in making the lift was stressed and fatigued, blood actually rushing to the muscle from other parts of the body to compensate for the effort. Actually, he didn't feel bad, not one bit.

"Hey, I'll be spotting for my man here." Tyrone had a gigantic grin on his face as always, an attitude that seemed to encourage everyone in the weight room. "We'd be stacking on another twenty. Seems my man here needs a real challenge." His voice rang out with enthusiasm and attracted some of the other players over in his direction as he slipped on the two ten-pound plates.

Richie repositioned himself and moved through another ten repetitions, the last three becoming progressively more difficult. He sat up and noticed how his arms seemed like they had a mind of their own. Instead of being able to easily raise them, they wanted to remain hanging at his sides like soft noodles.

"Shake it out, RJ," Tyrone instructed as he slipped on another ten-pound ring at each end of the bar. "Take your time. Rotate those shoulders and shake out those arms." Tyrone was acting out what he was describing to Richie, wanting him to mimic his actions.

Again, Richie positioned himself on the bench, grasped the bar, and lifted. It was ninety-five pounds, more than his body weight. He lowered and raised the bar through eight reps. His arms began to feel like they were going numb, and there was this prickly sensation in the biceps and the muscle or, at least, what he thought might be muscle in his chest. Then there was the sensation that his arms would collapse, the bar and weight enough, he thought, to slice him in half.

"Two more, RJ," Tyrone said with encouragement while the others who had gathered around shouted out words of support.

"Come on, nine and then ten." Tyrone placed his hands around the bar and guided the bar upward with a steady slight tug on the last two reps. "Good going, my man."

Richie lay on the bench, out of breath. How could lifting ninety-five pounds ten times be so exhausting, he thought as he tried to sit up but recognizing that even his stomach muscles were exhausted from the effort. He shook out the numbness in his arms and then tried again, finally rising to a sitting position on the bench. It was ninety-five pounds, ten times, a total of 950 pounds. Then he thought to himself, it was almost one-half of a ton, twice as much as a black bear might weigh, the weight of a race horse, one-half the weight of a female elephant. He now knew what the "burn" meant, and he instinctively rotated his shoulders and shook out his arms, trying to regain the sensation that his arms were actually attached to his body.

"Good set of reps. Good job, RJ." Several of the other players patted him on his shoulder as they spoke.

"Hey, my man." Tyrone slapped him on the back. "Good job, but now we do some legwork and some work with the dumbbells."

He smiled as he spoke, and Richie liked being around him, liked being around him more than any of the others, even though all of them treated him like part of the club rather than an assistant. Richie smiled at the others and nodded as they complimented him. But it was as if Tyrone, Speed as everyone called him, and Richie had something in common.

Speed and Richie worked first at the leg press machine and then did some arm curls followed by some abdominal crunches. Tyrone did his set, and then after removing most of the weights, Richie mimicked his actions. Richie wondered what it was that they shared in common, and then it suddenly dawned on him. Richie was small, real small, tiny compared to everyone else in the room. In the matter of size, he was very different from everyone else in the room, smaller than everyone in his class, the only half-pint anywhere in the area. And Tyrone was black, the only black player in the club, and, as far as Richie knew, the only black player on the team, maybe even in the school. They were both different from everyone else in the room, everyone in the school—Richie a pip-squeak compared to the others and Tyrone, black, black like charcoal, and in total contrast to any of the others. Then Richie thought that maybe, just maybe, it didn't matter, didn't matter to either of them that they were different from all the others. And it was because of that very fact that they were alike.

The shrillness of the coach's whistle brought the weight-lifting activity to a halt over the moans of the players. It was every other day that they finished their workouts with a series of staggered wind sprints that none of the players seemed to enjoy, no one except Tyrone. It was Tyrone who would almost effortlessly breeze from the baseline at the edge of the gym floor out to the first solid line and then back. The process would be repeated out and back to other solid lines running across the floor until the final leg was a gym long sprint out across the floor and back. As the players lined up, Richie turned to start picking up the towels, replacing the weights in the racks and cleaning up the weight room.

"Hey, Small." Coach Learner's voice echoed an unusual command. "We're waiting."

Richie looked in the coach's direction, turned to see what it was that he must have missed among the weight-lifting equipment, and then faced Learner with a puzzled look upon his face.

The expression on Learner's face seemed serious. "Are you a part of this club, or aren't you?"

"Coach Learner. . ." Richie started to respond, not knowing what he had done wrong.

"We lift, and then we run." A smile crossed Learner's face. "And that includes you, Small." Learner pointed in his direction.

"Come on, RJ. Let's get started," some of the players said in unison. "Get on over here, will you?"

A large grin crossed Richie's face as he scampered over toward the players. Tyrone motioned him over to the middle of the line where he stood just as the whistle sounded and the noise of squeaking tennis shoes suddenly echoed through the gym.

Richie had watched them run the drill on several other occasions and started out with the group running to the first line. As they returned to the baseline, having completed the first leg, Tyrone was already in front with Slant

and five or six of the other players, including the team captain leader being fairly close. As they did the second leg, the
bigger linemen struggled and fell further behind with the
second grouping starting to string out over the floor, Slant
still the closest to Tyrone. The gap between Tyrone and the
others grew on the third leg, and it was then that Richie
recognized something. While his legs were shorter and he
had to take almost two steps to each of theirs, he could
move his legs faster than the others and make the change of
direction at each line almost effortlessly. Suddenly, on the
second part of the third leg, he found himself even with
Slant and then suddenly ahead when they turned. Slant
caught him on the longest leg down but relinquished any
advantage as Richie quickly turned for home and held
him off to finish second among all the players. Of course,
Tyrone had finished almost the length of the gym ahead of
him and stood at the end line, seemingly not even breathing hard.

"Again!" Coach Learner commanded as he blew the
whistle ten seconds after the last man had finished.

Up and back they went. Ten sets of sprints with Richie
finishing second, ahead of everyone else, but almost a full
length of the gym behind Tyrone.

As they finished, Head Coach Ball called Richie's over
to him. He handed him a slip of paper with a locker number and a combination on it. "Small, you'll find two sets of

club sweats and gym clothes in this locker. It is your responsibility that you turn one set in each night after workouts for them to be washed."

The coach then looked down at his only pair of shoes. "And you cannot be wearing those on the gym floor. What size do you wear?"

Richie didn't really know because it seemed like his mother always came home with a partially worn pair that fit. He simply hunched his shoulders in an expression of not knowing.

Somehow, Coach Ball sensed something in those hunched shoulders. "Well, you see Junior tonight down in the locker room." The coach was referencing the older gentleman who served as the equipment manager. "Have him figure out your size. Tomorrow there will be two pairs of shoes in your locker, one for here and, well, just another pair for you."

Richie did not know what new shoes felt like, and the idea of having workout gear like the others made him feel special inside. He peered up at Ball, the words finally coming out of his mouth. "Thank you, thank you, Mr. Ball." As he finished, Tyrone placed his arm over his shoulder and led him away with the rest of the club down into the locker room.

The two men were the only ones who remained in the gym.

"Nice boy," Jeff Ball said to his assistant. "My first impression, though, was that this boy will never be a football player. How did you know that he had such speed?"

"I didn't," Learner responded.

"Well then, why did you choose him out of all the others in the middle school? He sure doesn't look like a future football player, probably the smallest kid in the school."

"He is going to be a three-year starter for us, Jeff, maybe a safety, or even a linebacker."

"Well, he'll have to beef up to play linebacker."

"Oh, he will. Mark my words, he will make both of us proud," Learner stated confidently.

"What makes you say that? What made you pick him out of the entire bunch?" Ball asked again.

Bob Learner looked out in the direction of the locker room and remembered when, not too many years ago, coaches had called him too small and, when someone signaled him out, gave him a special chance. He spoke the words with a sense of affection. "Because the boy has heart, Jeff. That boy has heart, tremendous heart, that will make him one of our best, and that's something you just can't teach a person."

CHAPTER 14

THE BOY AND the dog had become inseparable. On the weekdays, they were together every moment Richie was not in school. Working in and around their home, doing homework, or just playing in the yard, the dog and the boy were seemingly joined by some sort of invisible chain. If Richie was doing his homework, the dog was at his feet under the table. If he was watching television, she was at the side of the chair, or they were lying on the floor together. If reading in bed, she strategically placed herself across his feet.

Still, Richie recognized that the dog needed more than just being with him. He found an old tennis ball out by the playground one day, and that afternoon, he realized how much the dog enjoyed chasing that ball. At first, he would throw it anywhere in the yard, and the dog would race after it, oftentimes snatching it out of midair before it had finished even its first complete bounce. Then he would toss it into the cornfield, the dog diving in between the partially harvested stalks and quickly returning with the prized possession in her mouth. It was then that he recognized how the dog used her sense of smell to locate an object. When close enough to observe her, he could hear the rapid deep pounding sounds that emanated from deep inside her boxy snout. Even as she reached the ball, she made the final decision that she had found what she was seeking by taking a sharp sniff before gently snapping it up between her jaws.

On rainy days or just when he felt too lazy to take her outdoors, Richie realized that she enjoyed searching for the ball anywhere he could possibly hide it inside. Buried in the corner of the closet, inside the clothes dryer, in a closed drawer, or stuffed in between the pillows of the sofa, the dog, upon command, would set out on a patterned search based on her sense of smell that would lead her to the hidden object. Even when Richie placed the ball in the refrigerator, the dog would ultimately stand at the white door, look intently at the porcelain box, offer a single sharp bark, wait for the door to be opened, and then snap the ball off the shelf. Wherever she went, the dog would have the ball gently grasped in her jaws, that is unless Richie uttered the simple phrase, "Drop it." On command, the dog would let the object fall from her mouth at Richie's feet.

On the weekends, they had the luxury of being together the entire Saturday and Sunday if at home or in the village.

Richie had discovered the treasures of the Eureka Springs Public Library, and on Saturdays or Sundays, when his mother was working, the boy, the dog, and the almost perfectly smooth resemblance of a tennis ball literally ran into town together. And Richie had discovered the joy of running, especially after Coach Ball and Coach Learner continually encouraged him with comments about his speed. Donning his blue sweat suit embossed with the Panther script across the chest, the two of them would run to the library, the dog content to patiently wait on the front porch, ball still in her mouth, while her master searched for more words to consume.

On the winter days when the sun made it almost comfortable to stroll down the main street of the village, they would occasionally pass by the hardware, the three car dealerships, the pharmacy, either of the two small grocery stores, and other stores and study what was displayed in the windows. The boy would always cordially respond to those who offered a greeting or desired to pet the dog. He still felt separate from those in the community, including the other students in his class and school. If he considered anyone his true friend, it was several of the members from the weight and conditioning club, and especially Tyrone Walker. Walker and he had developed a special bond, even though six years separated their ages. Maybe it was the fact that both of them felt different from the others in the school.

Then there was his teacher, Mrs. Learner, with whom he had to contend. Ever since he had avoided the detention by inadvertently exposing a side of himself that he had carefully hidden from the other students, the fifth-grade teacher was slowly making more demands on him. He realized that he had allowed her to uncover his best kept secret. Then there was the morning when he found a book in his desk with a note on the first page suggesting that it might be something he would find interesting. He didn't do any better at concealing his abilities when, after reading it, he returned the 240-page novel just two days later. That same day, when she requested that he bring his lunch back to the room to eat and peppered him with questions about what he had just read, he realized that he had fallen into her nicely set trap. Yet it was the first time he was sharing something he enjoyed with someone other than his mother, and it made him feel real special.

Another book followed the first with a set of questions clipped to the first page. Then another, this a bit more difficult, no, a lot more difficult to both read and comprehend. At another session at lunch, he was asked to share his opinions about the book with Sarah Beamer. It was then that he discovered that it was a novel that had been assigned in a high school literature class that the always smiling aide was also reading. He realized that his secret, the fact that he was smart, was now known to both Mrs. Learner and the always smiling Sarah. But for the very first time, he really did not mind that they knew.

This particular Saturday was clear and crisp. So with the dog, the ball in her mouth at his side, Richie ran the three miles into Eureka Springs. On Main Street, he slowed to a walk and examined the various things in some of the storefront windows. As he passed the hardware store, he stopped and looked at the bicycles in the corner of the large display window. He had never owned a bike and, for that matter, never even ridden one. He looked at the thin tires and pondered the difficulty one would have in balancing on their very first attempt. His thoughts were interrupted by one of the employees exiting the front door and pushing another snowblower to the line of others sitting on the edge of the sidewalk.

"Nice dog you have there, young man. Is she friendly?" the man asked as he positioned the snowblower next to the others.

"Yes, sir," Richie answered politely.

The man squatted and patted his hand on the top of his thigh. "How you doing, girl?" He smiled and reached out to pet her as the dog approached, wagging her tail from side to side.

"Nice sweats you're wearing there." The man was referring to the blue hooded parka with the word *Panthers* embossed across the front in bright yellow. "You a member of the conditioning club that the football players have in the off-season?"

"No, sir." Richie responded. "Actually, I'm the student assistant, sir."

The man smiled back at him while he vigorously petted the dog along the top of the head and neck. "Hey, what does she have in her mouth?" he asked.

"Just her old ball," Richie answered. "As long as I allow her, she takes it everywhere we go." Richie positioned himself at the dog's side and spoke out a command in his normal voice. "Drop it here, Lady."

At the completion of his command, the dog turned her head and gently dropped the ball into Richie's open hand. He momentarily held the almost oblong piece of chewed rubber and then placed the ball in the pocket of his sweatpants. "Good girl." Richie patted the dog on the head.

"Hey, I've got something in here. Wait for a second."

The man retreated into the store and was back holding a clear plastic tube that contained three of the greenest, most perfectly round, and totally fuzz-covered tennis balls Richie had ever seen. With a gentle tug, he pulled the metal lid off the top of the tube. The accompanying swoosh of the vacuum seal being broken caused Lady to turn her head in the direction of the strange sound and pick up her ears in anticipation.

"Dog like yours there needs a better ball than whatever you put in your pocket." The man reached down and handed Richie the bright green sphere.

"Sir, but I don't have any money." Richie looked up at the man.

The man only smiled. "Here." He bounced the ball in front of Richie and the dog. Lady turned and snatched the ball out of midair. The man replaced a rubber lid on the tube containing the remaining two balls. "Just be taking storage space till spring." He smiled and ran the plastic tube into the pouch in the front of Richie's parka, patted the dog on the head, and turned back into the store.

"Sir. . ." There was a sense of urgency in Richie's voice, and the man stopped and looked back. "Sir, sir, thank you."

The man smiled and walked away.

Richie turned up Main Street and continued down to School Street where the Eureka Springs Public Library was located. The building was an accumulation of additions that protruded at odd angles from the original stone structure. It could only be entered over a large cement porch that ran the full length of the front of the building. Several metal benches were strategically placed across the porch and remained obviously unoccupied in the clear crisp weather of winter. With a simple command of "Stay!" Lady lay down in front of the bench nearest the entryway to the books that lay beyond its threshold. There she would remain until Richie returned.

Inside the building, Richie went first to the array of new titles that were exhibited on a tall four-sided stand in front of the checkout desk. Nothing seemed to appeal to him. In fact, some of the paper jackets covering the hardcover books exhibited scenes that would probably prove too adult-orientated for a fifth grader. He tried not to look, but the temptation forced him to glance. The dress on the pretty dark-haired woman on the cover of one of the selections seemed to be held in place only by a single strap that was precariously hanging onto the tip of her shoulder. *Obviously inappropriate for such a place as refined as a public library*, Richie thought.

He wound his way over to the History section and started thumbing through books on the Civil War. A book about the battle of Gettysburg snared his attention. Then a book on the battle of ironclad vessels supposedly designed to change the outcome of the Civil War piqued his curiosity. He took both and turned toward the back of the building and to a small alcove where two comfortable chairs were located and in which he knew he could curl into and read. As he hurried to the unoccupied of the two large chairs, he turned and came face-to-face with Tyrone Walker sitting in the other.

"Hey, RJ, what be happening, my good man?" Tyrone said quietly as he conspicuously laid down what he was reading and placed a sporting magazine over the top of the book.

Richie swallowed hard. Although there was this bond between Tyrone and him, it really had only existed in connection with the club. "I just picked up some books to read." He spoke back through a smile. "My mother works on Saturdays, and after I finish my chores, I come into town with Lady, and I spend some time in the library."

"They let your dog in here?" Tyrone asked, looking around while simultaneously moving the book that was now under the magazine further from Richie's view.

Tyrone's actions were not unnoticed. *Hey*, Richie thought, maybe he had picked up one of those books on the new arrival shelve, the ones with women with their dresses about to fall to the floor. It was none of his business; besides, he was in high school.

"No, Lady is on the porch. She will wait there until I come out," Richie responded.

Richie read the titles to Tyrone. "I think this one will be real interesting." He passed one of the books across the table that was between them. "The Monitor and the Merrimac were two ironclad vessels. See, the Confederates needed something that could help defeat the blockade of their ports. The Union Navy cut off most of their imports.

Without being able to export things like cotton, the Confederacy was desperate for a source of money as well as guns and ammunition from Europe."

"So you already read this here book?" Tyrone inquired.

Richie nodded his head no.

"Well then, how do you know all about the blockade and stuff like that?'

"I read the C volume of the encyclopedia, about the Civil War," Richie stated matter-of-factly, knowing that again he was saying too much but somehow feeling that he could share this with Speed.

"You did what?" Speed replied. "But why?'

Richie shrugged his shoulders. "Because it was interesting to read all that stuff."

Tyrone picked up the book and thumbed through it. He stopped at the middle of the book to peruse the pictures. "How long will it take you to read all this? Like, there are over three hundred pages, not counting the pictures."

"I don't know, maybe three or four days," Richie responded. "But today I was just going to pick through them and read some of the interesting stuff, things that caught my eye."

"You must have had some pretty good teachers to have you reading like that. I don't expect there are many other, what, fifth graders reading stuff like this?"

Richie shrugged his shoulders again. "I really don't know about what they read. I don't talk much with them."

There was a forlorn sound in Richie's voice, and Tyrone had noticed it. "Hey, I think it's great that you can read things like this. Anyway, who cares what they think."

Richie liked talking with the black high school football star. He attempted to extend the conversation. "I bet you read a lot of books like this in high school, books about the Civil War, probably the Revolutionary War too. History is always so interesting. . ." He stopped as he watched Tyrone's thoughts drift off to somewhere else.

After several long moments, Richie wondered if he should break the silence that had surrounded them. "Is everything okay?"

There was no longer the always present smile on his face. "How did you learn to read like this? Who taught you?" Tyrone asked.

Richie pondered the question. "Well, I guess my mother. She taught me. At least, she started teaching me. She read to me every day. I remember sitting on her lap, and she would read to me. Then I guess I started reading simple books, and then we would read together. We still read together, at least, when she is home. More so when we were back in Kentucky, but with her working as much as she does now, we just haven't had the time."

Tyrone was now staring at him across the table. He hesitated and then started, finally sputtering out the words. "Do you. . .do you think she could teach someone else, teach me to read?"

Richie did not answer but just peered back at the face across from him, his silence demanding an explanation.

The powerful-looking football player, the sure-to-be state champion in probably both the one-hundred-meter and two-hundred-meter sprints, next season's all-state, maybe all-American football player reached into his coat pocket and laid open a piece of paper in front of Riche.

"Do you know what this means?" Tyrone's voice started out firm but ended with an emotional quiver. "Those grades will mean I will probably be ineligible by this spring and for sure next fall."

Richie looked first at the report card and then back at Tyrone.

"See, back in Mississippi, I seemed to get away with it. I could fake most of it maybe because no one cared." There was an expression of sadness spreading across his face. "They all knew it, they all knew I couldn't read, but what did they care? Who gave a damn about some black kid bouncing around from family to family, his mama off somewhere and no father? Who cared about some stupid ass black kid. . .?" The statement seemed to be incomplete, but Tyrone fell into a stupefied silence.

Somehow, the silence between them was like a pounding in his head. He liked Tyrone, he liked him because, like Richie, he was different; like Richie, he had hidden something; like Richie, he was alone among those around him.

For only the second time, for the second time since he yelled at Frank Savage to get out of their home, Richie became assertive. He reached around the table and to the material on the floor and removed the book from under the sporting magazine. On the book in his hands were the words: Dick and Jane.

Tyrone pointed to the cover of the book. "First-grade crap, real genius, aren't I? Nothing but a stupid ass loser."

Richie was shocked by the language. Why, he wondered, would he say such an awful thing, especially about himself? Then it dawned on him. "So you can read."

"If you call that reading."

He looked sternly into his face. "I do," Richie replied, knowing that when he was in the weight room lifting less than one hundred pounds rather than three hundred pounds that the players were lifting, he was still lifting.

"Then that's where we start, build up from there, just like in the weight room." Richie's statement was in the form of a demand, and as he made it, all kinds of ideas ran through his head.

He thought about Coach Learner but realized that for now, Tyrone meant this to be a secret. He wondered about some special type teacher, but whom? There was Mrs. Learner, she shared the same passion for reading as Richie, and besides, she was good at keeping secrets. Suddenly, it dawned on him—his mother, she would help. And there was Sarah Beamer, another person Richie had grown to trust. There was a treasure trove of people, and unexpectedly he included himself.

"First, my mother and I can help," Richie stated.

"But no teachers!" Tyrone responded.

"No teachers." Richie agreed for the moment. "Look, you come over to my place tonight around seven. My mother will be home a bit later, after the dinner shift."

"You'll help me, you and your mother?" Tyrone's statement was blunt.

"Why, sure, why not?" Richie asked.

"Because I'm black, black and stupid."

The statement hurt Richie because he recognized how it felt to be different. Suddenly, he stated what was in his heart. "Because you are a friend and you need our help."

After they had made their plans and Tyrone had left the library, Richie thought about what he needed. He searched the children's section and found several books for which there was more than one copy. Selecting three sets of two, he went to the desk in an attempt, for the very first time, to check out books from the Eureka Springs Public Library.

"I'd like to check out these books, please," he said in the direction of the horn-rimmed spectacles that were precariously balanced on the end of the elderly woman's nose standing behind the counter.

The irises of her eyes were magnified by the thickness of her glasses and appeared as two deep pools of black that seemed to reflect Richie's face back at him, especially when she spoke. "Your library card, please."

Richie cleared his throat. "I don't have one."

The woman's voice was quiet but authoritative. "Library cards can be issued at no charge for those living within the village limits and for a minimal yearly payment of five dollars for those residing in the township." She looked down at Richie. "What is your address, young man?"

The numbers on the trailer had been obliterated a long time ago, and Richie could only respond. "We live out past Townline and before Cumberland."

"Township," the woman said bluntly as she passed him a form. "Complete this form and include a five-dollar payment for the necessary card."

Richie did not know what to say. He could not argue, especially with someone who probably knew everything there possible was about obtaining a library card. He was about to return the books to their proper shelf when the voice of a woman interrupted his action.

"I'll vouch for the boy and get him his card, Mrs. Reid." The voice was directed to the librarian, and it was soft but firm, a voice he recognized.

Richie turned to face Mrs. Learner.

"See you discovered our public library." There was this wonderful smile running across her face. "I knew you eventually would." She had withdrawn a five-dollar bill from the purse balanced on a heap of books. "Do you come here often?"

The response came from Mrs. Reid. "Saturdays and sometimes on Sundays for the last several weeks."

It seemed like those spectacles saw everything, Richie thought. "Mrs. Learner, I can't take your money," Richie responded as she handed the money to Mrs. Reid.

"Nonsense," Mrs. Learner stated, her beautiful smile becoming even broader as she passed a pen to Richie to complete the application. "See, Richard, you have a special talent, a passion for reading." She spoke softly and directly to him as if there were no classmates to share what was being said. "We share that passion, Richard, and it is a tool that opens up the entire wonderful world right before your very eyes."

She paused. "What have you got there?" Mrs. Learner inquired. "Trying to help someone to learn to read?"

It was true, Richie thought, teachers, if you are not careful, can read your mind. Then he noticed how the sets of books were sprawled over the counter. He completed the application without responding, and as Mrs. Learner checked out her books, they turned to walk out of the library together.

Again, it seemed as if she knew what he was thinking. "It is a good technique. I've used it myself. What you will want them to do is read along with you at first. Then as they become more adept, have them read to you, first sentences, then paragraphs, then an entire page, and then pretty soon the chapter." She paused. "I did not know you had a younger sister or brother at home."

"I don't," Richie replied again, recognizing how Mrs. Learner seemed to gain information with such simple statements.

They stopped on the front porch where Richie was greeted by Lady.

"My husband mentioned you had a pet," Mrs. Learner stated.

It was confirmed, finally confirmed, Coach Learner was Mrs. Learner's husband, not a brother. Somehow, Richie was glad with the conclusion.

"I'll tell you what," Mrs. Learner began, "all the other students have given an oral presentation to the class, fifteen minutes about a hobby, special interest, or talent, all the other students but you and Abe Lastly." She smiled down at Richie.

"How about we make a deal?" she stated. "For the five dollars, you make an oral presentation next Friday about your dog here, and then we can keep Abe happy by allowing him to bring up the rear as always."

The fear that crossed his face must have been as obvious as the red of Principal Glum's bow tie firmly sandwiched between his puffy white chin and starched white shirt. But somehow, he cleared the lump that seemed to run from his belt buckle to the back of his tongue and belched out the letters "OK."

"Next Friday it is then," Mrs. Learner stated as she started walking down the steps. Then she turned back in his direction. "And I'll tell you what, I'll make arrangements with the school to allow your dog in for the day. How does that sound?"

Richie still could not properly respond, but his hesitation allowed for Lady, as if knowing what was said, to chime in with a firm bark.

Now Richie stood on the steps of the library, thinking of what had happened. A simple trip to the library, and suddenly he is going to tutor Tyrone Walker. But worse yet, he would have to make an oral presentation in front of his entire fifth-grade class. As he thought about all that had just happened, Lady nudged her snout into his hand, and he felt the furry cover of the new tennis ball in her mouth. The day was not an entire disaster. At least, Lady had a set of three new tennis balls.

CHAPTER 15

I T HAD NOT been as easy as he had thought. While the two of them had sat across from each other for the better part of an hour reading from the same two books, Richie could see little progress. At first, Richie had read three or four sentences out loud and then had Tyrone read the next sentence. The improvement, if any, was not noticeable as Tyrone struggled with almost every word. He tried reading almost the entire page aloud, having the best football player on the Eureka Springs Panthers football team try to finish the last sentence. In this manner, he hoped that some of the words would be repetitive and, therefore, recognizable. Still, his friend barely stumbled along, frustrated by his inability.

Lady lifted her head and stared out as if she could see through the thin wall of the trailer. The slamming of a car door alerted Richie that his mother was home. It would be no surprise that someone would be visiting since the white four-door sedan was also parked in the driveway.

"Hi, Mom," Richie said as he got up from his chair at the kitchen table and helped with some items wrapped tightly in her arms.

A gust of wind blew by the trailer, and Becka Small turned to pull the dilapidated outer door shut. "Richie, who is. . ."

His response cut off her statement. "A friend, one of the football players from the club is here." He placed the items he had taken from her on the counter. "I'm helping him with some of his schoolwork."

Becka swiveled toward the person and came face-to-face with Tyrone. Her face suddenly wore a suspicious stare, a combination of surprise and concern, and she stopped in her tracks. She anticipated a student, someone from the conditioning club, but the deep blue black of the teenager in front of her drew a sense of concern across her face. In Louisville, she had become very accustomed to blacks in the city, many well-to-do and dining at the fine restaurant where she worked.

In Kentucky, from where she had come, while the community was equally represented, it had remained divided. The whites in the community frequently reverted to slurs and jokes that most often masked their own shortcomings. She did not participate in that type of talk, but its prevalence had a way of blemishing what could be good about a community. In her house in the middle of Michigan, it was a surprise because she had never seen a black person in Eureka Springs. With it came an expression that she was unable to conceal.

Tyrone sensed apprehension. The bewildered look on someone's face was something he had become accustomed to since coming to the small village. He stood up and politely smiled at her. "Mrs. Small, my name is Tyrone Walker." His voice was exceedingly polite.

Becka regained her composure, looked first at her son and back at the stranger in her home.

"Tyrone needs some help, Mom. I told him that I could help him, you and me, we could."

Becka was only nodding her head but with a befuddled look on her face.

"Maybe I should go, RJ." Tyrone began to pick up the material in front of him.

"No, no, of course not." She sputtered out the words, realizing that she had embarrassed him. "Anyway, my car is the last one in the driveway. No, a friend of Richie's. . ." She recalled her son saying friend. "A friend of Richie's is always welcome." A pleasant smile had replaced the confused expression. "In fact, I have brought some food home from the restaurant. You will stay and join us for dinner."

"Great, Mom! We're both hungry," Richie stated excitedly. "Then I can tell you all about what we plan on doing."

Becka Small stepped forward. "Richie has talked about some of you, some of the members of the club, that is." She suddenly realized that her work schedule had allowed so little time for them to really discuss the matter. All she really knew was that it seemed to be something that her son really enjoyed.

"Well, RJ is really something else. Everyone really likes him, Mrs. Small. He truly is a fine gentleman," Tyrone stated.

"RJ?" Becka questioned.

"Oh, they call me RJ, just like Tyrone's nickname is Speed, Mom. Speed is the best running back in the conference, maybe in the state. He is going to be the state hundred-meter champion too," Richie stated.

"RJ, well, I prefer Richie," Becka responded as she looked over at the newcomer in her home. "And, young man, would you mind if I keep things a little more traditional and call you by your Godgiven name?"

"Not at all, ma'am."

Becka moved into the kitchen and placed the rest of the items she carried on the counter. She turned back in his direction. "And a friend of Richie's is always welcome for dinner, even if it is some of today's specials that most of our customers just didn't think as being that special." Her demeanor was more comfortable. "Spaghetti and tossed salad, some Italian bread, nothing too extravagant."

Richie quickly cleared the books from the kitchen table as Becka rearranged the items that had been placed on the counter.

"If you give me ten minutes, I will have this all warmed up," Becka stated.

"May I help with something, Mrs. Small?" Tyrone asked.

"Of course not." She smiled back in his direction. "You're our guest."

As she set the table, Becka voiced her curiosity. "What exactly is it that Richie is helping you with, Tyrone?"

"Well, it is kind of embarrassing." He sputtered through the reply. "See, I know Richie is a good reader. I've seen him come and go from the library the last few Saturdays."

Richie's face had a look of surprise on it as Tyrone spoke. The only occasion that he could recall seeing him there was that very afternoon.

"Your son is real special, Mrs. Small," he continued. "It is almost like he eats through the words like a hungry squirrel at a full bird feeder. I've seen him go through an entire book, two books, in an afternoon, too busy to even notice that I was watching him."

Becka had turned from the plates she was setting on the table and toward him. Suddenly, a high school student and a fifth grader with two of the same books made sense to her. She peered back at him as he continued.

"I can't read. Well, just barely. See, I moved up here from Mississippi, and well, down there they didn't care if I could read or not. Who cared about some stupid kid jumping from school to school? I wasn't in any one school long enough for anyone to find out, even if they did care about some stupid black kid with no ma or pa." His voice began to break."

His description of such a travesty added a continuing sense of pain.

"Anyway, when my ma took off, I mean for good, she was never really around much anyway. No one really cared where I ended up, that is until my aunt, actually my great-aunt, found out." He looked up at her as he finished. "And now here I am living here in Eureka Springs over on Busch Road."

He sputtered through the embarrassment of the explanation and then stopped for a long moment, and there was almost a pleading in his voice. "And I just thought Richie could help me."

She carefully studied him before speaking. Somehow, she knew what the answer would be if she inquired if he had asked his teachers for help. He was embarrassed, feeling very different, the inability making him an outcast. Then too he was black, probably the only black person in the entire school. She understood, just like she understood how Richie felt in a new community, how he felt different because they were poor, how he felt different because he had no father, and how he felt different because he was small.

Several moments had passed as she reflected, a serious look forming across her face as she gazed out at the two people standing in front of her. "You two come and sit down." She turned back to what she was doing. "We'll eat, and then we can start." She had a stern look on her face. "It is going to involve a lot of hard work, and we'll start right after dinner."

The two boys came to the table. Richie sat down, and for an awkward moment, Tyrone stood behind the chair across from her. "I'm sorry, Mrs. Small. Maybe I shouldn't be asking this of Richie. Maybe I should go to the counselor or one of my teachers."

She was nodding her head no, knowing what he must be going through. "You're not asking Richie, you're asking the two of us. Let's see what we can accomplish first. You two sit down and eat, and then we'll get to work."

He sat down and then looked up at Becka. "Thank you, Mrs. Small." His voice dripped with sincerity.

CHAPTER 16

FRIDAY HAD COME faster than Richie desired. Speaking in front of the class was something that he had avoided here in Eureka Springs as well as back in Kentucky. It just drew too much attention. And attention was something to be avoided. It was like walking by a house where there is a dog that bites, Richie thought. It is best to try and stay totally unnoticed. Because once you're noticed, there are plenty of things that could go wrong. The leash could be untied, the collar could be loose and come off, the gate open, the owner somewhere else, a tree not close enough to climb, or a door not near enough to hide behind. The options were all bad.

Richie felt the same way about giving a presentation. It always seemed like it hurt, especially if you were poor, living only with a mother, wearing big thick glasses more often than not held together with white tape, living in a run-down trailer, and being the smallest person in the class.

Someone always had something to say that would bite, not like a mean dog but inside, inside of you where it really hurt.

He had thought about bringing her to school on the bus but didn't even bother asking. Mr. Glum would have surely put the old Glum kibosh to the idea by his typical indirect statement, "Well, what do you think, Mr. Small?" It was not meant as a question because he was the man in charge, and everyone recognized it.

Instead, Richie would jog to school that day past the bus stop, along the country road, and down the steep hill that led into Eureka Springs. He did it on Saturdays and Sundays, why not on a school day?

He had mentioned what he was doing to Tyrone on Wednesday after the club workout and while at the trailer immersed in a reading lesson. And then on Thursday after school, Captain Leader and Tyrone approached him with an idea. Little did he know that some of the members of the club ran to school several days a week, including Captain and Speed. They crossed Cumberland just down from Townline, but it would be just as easy to turn up Cumberland and pick Richie up on the way. And that is how it was decided he would get the dog to school.

He and Lady stood at the foot of the driveway two hundred yards up from the four corners and the bus stop. The others had gathered to catch the bus as usual, Goodfellow holding court with some of his subjects. On this day, a newcomer was at the stop. A big black Mercedes had pulled up and stopped at the street leading into the subdivision of large homes and dropped off a pretty fifth grade girl. As she walked up toward the corner, Clarence was doing his best to impress, impress by intimidation.

He never touched the girls and seldom made fun of them unless it was behind their back and mostly to other boys who seemed to care. The blubbery sixth grader was just about ready to threaten one of his subjects with an in-the-armpit headlock when he noticed Richie walking toward them from his driveway.

"Hey, Smallie, you runnin' away from that there trailer of yours, you and that mangy dog?" he bellowed out the statement as Richie approached the corner. It did not impress the others since even in the distance, they saw the blue parka with the word *Panthers* scrawled across the front.

"Yeah, I'd be running away too if I were you." Clarence was desperate to put Richie in his place. It seemed that the punch to the midsection had loosened the royal grip that he had on his subjects, even though Richie had experienced the "royal dunkin'," as Clarence put it.

"Must stink in that old tin can of yours." Clarence was relentless as he gargled out more words.

A couple other sixth graders rewarded Clarence with several chuckles, and it egged him on.

"What you waiting for, Mr. Panther?" Clarence referenced the script across the parka. "What, a panther is a cat, isn't it? That's right, a cat, you and the dog, a little puddie cat and a dog. Meow, meow, come here, little puddie cat."

Unnoticed to Clarence as he taunted Richie, others in hooded parkas were quickly approaching from the east. They ran in unison, long strong legs pounding out a rhythm on the shoulder of the road. They were at the corner before Clarence even noticed.

"Hey, RJ my man, how we doing?" The comment came from the black runner in the group of three, his spoken words fluttering through the puff of gray that accompanied his breathing in the cold winter air.

"Hey, Speed, Captain, Slant," Richie responded nonchalantly as the three runners momentarily slowed and repositioned themselves, the black runner moving slightly ahead of the others so Richie could run alongside him.

Then the pace was resumed, the four runners pounding out a fast jog down the road, the dog looping effortlessly at Richie's side. As they crossed the road to the subdivision, two other boys ran out onto the road and fell in behind the others, the black runner, Richie, and the dog still in the lead.

Each member of the assembled group at the corner watched, their eyes focused on the steady rhythm of the runners. The boys waiting for the bus were envious, each wanting to be part of the conditioning club no matter what type of joke Clarence attempted to make.

"Who are they?" the new girl asked one of the other girls.

"They are some of the players of the Eureka Springs Panther football team." Clarence proclaimed the answer. "Conference champions for seven years running and been in the playoffs, state championship finals too. I'm gonna be playing varsity football my freshman year." Clarence boasted.

"And the boy with the dog?" the girl again inquired.

Again, Clarence just had to answer. "That's tiny smelly Smallie nobody. You can call him Four Eyes if you want. Ain't nothin' but the dumbest little twerp in the fifth grade." Clarence giggled as if what he had said was funny.

The bus clamored up to the stop, and the children filed in. After another stop farther up Cumberland, the bus finally passed the group of runners, now totaling eleven all clad in the blue parkas with "Panthers" scrawled across the front. And as she looked out the window, the little blonde girl saw the boy with the dog, arms pumping, legs churning, the dog at his side, and still running at the head of the pack with another runner. A fifth grader, she thought, maybe he would be in her class, Mrs. Learner's class. At least, she hoped so as she prepared for her first day of school and Eureka Springs.

CHAPTER 17

THE FIRST TEST had come at the entrance of the middle school. Mr. Glum had his eyes focused out on the sidewalk, among the students departing the buses, others walking up the driveway, and still others getting out of cars in the designated area. Mr. Glum's eyes never darted from student to student, but somehow, he seemed to focus on everything and everyone at the very same time. It was either some type of genetic mutation or something practiced at principal school, Richie had concluded. And Richie felt the stare, among a hundred or so kids, felt Mr. Glum's focus in the middle of his forehead. It was like he was branding a spot right there above the bridge of his nose, and as he approached, the sensation burned as if a hot coal had been set directly above his eyes.

"And where do you think you are going with that, Mr. Small?" As always, Mr. Glum's statement had no questioning about it. He then pointed toward the Labrador that had attracted a bevy of hands trying to pet her.

Richie swallowed hard and tried to gather enough spit in his mouth to keep his words from being just a hot blowing sound crossing over his lips. And there was another reason to be concerned. Why did Mr. Glum know his name?

Richie looked up past the tightly cinched belt that was far closer to his neck than his navel over the hard-as-plaster, starched white shirt that seemed to blur your vision if you looked at it too long, past the brilliant red, like blood, bow tie, and up into the hairy nostrils of the principal that flared open as he spoke, as if stealing air from those around him. Richie carefully reached into his pocket and produced a slip of paper that Mrs. Learner had provided him, signed by her, Becka Small, and the superintendent of Eureka Springs Public Schools.

Mr. Glum looked at the paper, down at Richie, and then back to the official-looking document. He took a lot longer than he needed to study the note, almost as if he wanted to find something wrong. Finally, his nostrils flared open, and the response cascaded back down. "Well, there will be no accidents, Mr. Small."

"No, sir," Richie managed to reply, worried more about his potential for having an accident than Lady, especially if he had to stand in front of the class and speak for anything more than a minute.

Faced with the document and the correct signatures, Principal Glum had no alternative, so he nodded with his head toward the interior of the school and handed Richie back the note.

Before Richie could say thank you, Lady spun around, made an effortless leap into the air, gave one bark, and landed back next to Richie. It was if she too approved the gesture. But as they walked away, Richie turned and looked back at Mr. Glum. There on the back of his bone-white shirt was a single paw print as obvious as a pimple on the end of a nose. Now there was all the reason in the world to get as far away as possible from the vigilant Principal Glum.

Richie and Lady walked to his locker. The dog garnered all the attention, hands petting her on the head and students reaching out and touching the soft fur on her back. Even some of the older seventh and eighth grade boys displayed a playfulness that was in contrast with the self-assuredness they tried to exude since they were the oldest boys in the building. From every direction there came the comment, "Look at the puppy." Richie thought the comment funny because assuredly Lady was not a puppy. And while everyone spoke to the dog, no one spoke to or, for that matter, even noticed Richie.

In Mrs. Learner's classroom, Richie sat down at his desk, and Lady sprawled out next to him, her ears pricking upward and her deep dark eyes examining the children that surrounded her. The children swarmed over her, but she did not seem to care. A renewed wagging of her tail accompanied a deep powerful gaze into every different face. No one was paying any attention to anything but the dog, and being ignored was something with which Richie never had a problem.

Even with the presence of a dog, Mrs. Learner's entry into the classroom had all the children in their seats in a matter of a single moment. They quickly quieted down and attended to immediate business, that being the morning announcements from the office. It was all filtered through the speaker system, making Secretary Carla Loud sound as if she were talking from somewhere in outer space.

"Good morning, class." Mrs. Learner always started the workday out with the pleasantry. "Before we get busy today, I want all of you to welcome our new student." Mrs. Learner nodded toward the rear of the room where the pretty girl from the bus stop was sitting. In the early morning commotion involving the dog, even she was ignored.

"Her name is Tina Price, and she has just moved here from Atlanta, Georgia." Twenty-seven sets of eyes turned in unison and peered at the newcomer. "I would hope each of you would make her feel welcome, maybe help her find her way to the cafeteria and to her electives."

Mrs. Learner did her best to immediately assimilate the new student into the class. "But we are not going to allow her to sit in a row all by herself." She motioned to two of the boys. "Let's see, why don't we move that desk right over there. That will make it seven rows of four desks."

To Richie's consternation, Mrs. Learner was pointing to the open space created by there only being three desks in the back row, an open space that he had been able to create between him and Janice Wright, which he felt was just about right. After the boys moved her desk and filled up the extra space in the back row, the new girl timidly resumed her seat, trying to make as little eye contact with the others in the class as possible. But as she sat down, she momentarily looked in Richie's direction, and he noticed the smallest of smiles.

For Richie, the morning seemed to rocket toward the 10:10 bell that would signal recess and then the scheduled return to the classroom at 10:35. On this Friday, Richie Small would be the only student making an oral presentation to the class. It was as if recess was only a flash in his memory. Now back in the classroom, the second hand seemed to leap across the face of the clock, tearing off chunks of time and bringing Richie closer to his appointment with destiny.

For some reason, even the ever-smiling Sarah Beamer had come over from the high school to observe the presentation. Mrs. Learner made the introduction, and Richie rose, Lady at his side, and approached his impending embarrassment with downturned head and eyes focused on nothing but the carpeting on the floor. He stuttered and stammered through two sentences and paused. Giggles and partially hushed laughter twisted through the room.

Then while looking down, he met the stare from the tilted head of the animal next to him. There seemed to something magical in those deep almost-black eyes. The dog tilted his head the opposite way and refocused on the boy, the same look that the mangy animal had focused on a boy drenched in dirty water, standing on the other side of the road, who would become his best friend. She nudged his hand with her snout as if encouraging him on, telling him that this mattered to her too. And then Richie realized that he was describing her, his best friend, and that this was not about him.

Richie took a long pause and then started over. "Lady, that is the name of my yellow Labrador Retriever. Actually, she is a British Lab, there being two different standards of Labradors, British and American."

As he continued, he raised his head and looked toward the back of the room and then some of the faces in front of him. He recited much of what he had read, describing the different breeds, their temperament, their use—at first, as dogs for hunting waterfowl and then as dogs used to help the blind or the disabled. He spoke about how the British Labs were descendants from six remaining dogs obtained from a nobleman's estate in England in the late nineteenth century. He talked about the size of the typical litters, when pups were weaned, and how to best train a dog. He retold two stories about how such dogs had saved the lives of people, one a child lost in the woods and the other of a family trapped in a burning house.

The giggles and hushed comments had stopped after he restarted, and he quickly had the full attention of the students. For twenty-five minutes, without the help of a single note card, Richie at first interested and then mesmerized the twenty-seven other students and, for that matter, Mrs. Learner and Sarah. All this time, the dog sat at his side and watched him speak.

"Lady has another special skill," he continued. "Labradors have a keen sense of smell and oftentimes identify objects more by smell than sight."

Richie went on to describe how the dog would often identify her favorite object, her tennis ball, by smelling it before picking it up with her mouth and how the dog was able to locate the ball no matter where Richie would hide it. He described how the exceptional sensory perception of smell worked and that the breed was often used by law enforcement agencies for a variety of different chores. Then he suggested an experiment as he retrieved her tennis ball from his parka.

"If Mrs. Leaner would allow, we will go out into the hallway, and she can hide the ball anywhere in the room, and we will see how long it takes for Lady to find it." Richie suggested.

Mrs. Learner nodded her approval while Richie showed the dog the ball and allowed her to take it from his hand with her mouth. Then taking the ball back, he handed it to his teacher, and he and the dog left the room. The first experiment was an almost effortless chore, the dog entering the room, turning her nose into the air and to the ground, and dividing the room into four quarters while deep pulsating sounds came from her snout. She turned into one quarter and seemed to follow an invisible trail up to the desk, placed her forepaws on it, took a deep whiff of the green furry object, and then reached out and snatched the ball from next to the cup holding the teacher's pencils.

The students were enthralled by how the dog operated, and each had suggestions of where the ball could be hidden. But each time Richie and Lady reentered the room, other attempts to conceal the ball from the dog proved fruitless. In the corner, under the radiator, then in a closet, and then even in the empty tissue box in Cindy Colder's desk, the dog never failed. The more concealed, the more time it took, but Lady, her jowls slapping out the pulsating sounds, circled the room, sectioned it off, and then meticulously worked the area until the ball was discovered. The other students were awestruck by the dog's ability.

Then the timid voice of the new student voiced a question over the excitement of the others. "Can Lady find other things besides her ball?" she asked as the other classmates chimed in on the question.

Richie made eye contact directly with her. "Sure." Richie looked around for another object.

"How about my scarf?" Tina untied and held the yellow and red scarf she wore around her neck out to Richie.

Richie allowed Lady to smell the fabric and then gave the scarf back and departed the room. When the dog returned, she immediately went to work, moving across the room, her head darted from side to side and divided the room into two sections. She momentarily slowed at the desk where Tina was sitting, possibly confused by similar smells, and then moved toward the back of the room. Sniffing and pounding out that same noise from her snout, she quickly focused on the book bags in the back of the room and then one particular bag that she pawed at until Richie opened it. The class erupted in cheers as the bell for lunch sounded.

The typically growling stomachs of the students before lunch were ignored as everyone asked Richie to perform the experiment again. And Lady did, this time with Mrs. Learner's glass case. But the schedule dictated lunch, and the students reluctantly lined up to go to the cafeteria and then out for noon recess.

Richie, why don't you show our new student to the cafeteria?" Mrs. Learner stated as the others started to depart.

He looked down at the dog. "The instructions were that the dog could not go in the cafeteria, Mrs. Learner," Richie responded. "But I could eat my lunch here."

Mrs. Learner agreed as she turned toward the new student. "Tina, would you bring your lunch back so I can make sure you have all your textbooks and explain what you will have to do?"

Tina agreed, and as she did, Richie noticed that a smile had crossed her face. He thought he could feel comfortable around her, that they had something in common. Maybe it was because she was new or that she was from the south, from Georgia. Maybe it was because she was petite, a small thin girl with long blond hair and big round blue eyes and that she too was small in size. And then he realized that he had been staring at her.

The little girl from Georgia came over and petted Lady gently on the head. The dog nudged up against her legs. Then for some reason, Tina took the scarf from around her neck and tied it gently around the neck of the dog. She looked over at Richie. "Do you think Lady would like wearing a scarf?"

Richie paused and looked at the now yellow and red object adorning the dog's neck. It looked dumb, he thought, and was about to say no. But then he noticed the smile on

Tina's face and the sparkle in her eyes as she hugged the dog. And as Lady poured out those dark eyes back in his direction as if saying it was okay, Richie agreed.

At lunch and while Mrs. Learner was busy working with Tina, Richie surprised Sarah with a unique request as to her helping someone with their reading. He did not say whom he was helping, but Sarah gladly agreed.

At the end of the school day, Mrs. Learner suggested that Richie show Tina to her bus. They had exited the building and found Mrs. Driver behind the wheel of the venerable old yellow tub lined up with seventeen similar buses in the circle driveway of the middle school.

"This is it." It was the first words he had spoken to her since lunch, and even those were expressed with a reluctance. "You'll get off at the second stop at the corner up from the subdivision." He smiled at her, turned, and started walking away.

"Aren't you riding home?" she asked as she followed him down the sidewalk.

He motioned down with his head toward the dog. "Lady and I, well, we're walking home. It's only three miles." He marveled at how quickly he responded to her question.

Just then, the grandiose Clarence Goodfellow barged through the sea of kids, scrambling toward their assigned buses. Most of the others made way for his round frame.

Those unlucky enough not to get out of his way in time were jarred to the sides with just enough of his bulk to make it appear that he was not intentionally pushing. And anyway, it was the protruding belly or bulging hips, even the misshapen prominence of his massive thighs, and not his hands that he used to open the path for his travels.

Richie reached back and grabbed the unsuspecting new girl just as Clarence arrived, saving her from the discomfort of being jostled by jiggling fat.

"Gang way!" Clarence bellowed as he reached the first step. "I've got things to do and places to go." That false expression of timidity crossed his face as he encountered Mrs. Driver. "How are you today, Mrs. Driver?" The pleasantry in his voice suddenly dripped like sap from an open cut on a pine tree.

"Just get on, Goodfellow," she stated with an indication of disgust in her voice.

"That's someone you want to avoid," Richie said as he suddenly realized that he was still holding her by the wrist. He immediately dropped her arm.

"I thought so," Tina replied. "He made quite a spectacle of himself at the bus stop this morning." She turned her head toward the bus and then looked back at Richie. "Do you think I could walk home with you?" she asked. "I think you go right by my street."

A knot developed in Richie's throat, and it took a moment for the words to work themselves by it. "Yeah." He hesitated. "Yeah, sure. That would be nice."

Then Richie and Tina started down the driveway, out toward the grain elevator that would lead them up the hill and out of the village. Lady walked beside them, still wearing the colorful scarf around her neck that now so much seemed a part of her. And if anything, there appeared to be a dog smile upon her face.

CHAPTER 18

ALMOST TWO MONTHS had passed, and for Richie, it might have been the best weeks of his entire grade school life. First, school and everything that went with it was becoming something that he had started to enjoy. The players in the club had not only accepted Richie but also viewed him as a member rather than a student assistant. He worked hard helping, but what mattered most was that he was included in the conditioning as well as some distance running that the club members undertook.

Even if they didn't, he would run. Running had become a passion to him almost as important as his reading. He would run into town on the weekends, selecting different routes, circling out the other side of the village, down the country roads, even dirt two tracks, and then paths that wound through the rocky and forested hill country back along the north side of town.

It was the hill country that attracted him most. It was harsh and difficult terrain with the tall evergreens somehow protruding through the rocky outcrops and spots of yellow clays. Intermingled among the tall trees were the openings to some of the now empty pits and shallow mine shafts where soft coal deposits had been extracted in the late 1800s. Out under the pines, alone except for Lady, he liked running where there was no pavement, no houses, and no cars. He liked the sound of his shoes picking and choosing their path over and between the rocks and the rhythmic plying of his arms and legs that propelled him almost effortlessly along whatever course he would chose.

He went anywhere, feeling safe because Lady was always at his side. More than once, mean-looking dogs charged down driveways or through yards. Lady would bound out in their direction. Through a display of deep growls and intimating charges, she somehow communicated to her fellow canine that she and her master were not to be messed with. Others got to know the boy and the dog, and people would frequently wave as he passed, some even calling out his name, and the dog's only reaction to these people was the friendly wagging of her tail as she ran at his side.

The environment in the classroom had also changed. Others recognized that the student assistant position was something all the boys in the middle school coveted. And while no one discussed the matter, they all knew who that person was, at least for this year. Then there was the matter of Clarence Goodfellow. The thwarting of an attempted sock-oh by the simple fist squeezing by someone as recognized as Tyrone Walker had spread through the middle school faster than a fifth grader could find their homework in the mess inside their locker when threatened with a detention.

Clarence now steered clear of Richie for one obvious reason—ignoring him meant that hopefully the others would forget. First, it had been the punch in the belly and then the humiliation by Tyrone Walker. Maybe, for the first time in his life, Clarence Goodfellow was embarrassed. Others in his classroom, at first, displayed a friendlier attitude towards Richie, many inquiring about Lady. But as time passed, Richie fell comfortably into the background, happy to be left alone, left alone by everyone in the classroom except for one student.

Tina Price was special. Sure, she was a new student to Eureka Springs and a quiet little girl. She too liked to read almost as much as Richie. And she too desired as little attention as possible in the classroom. At first, Richie could not figure out why he felt the way he did. She was pretty, real pretty. Her blond hair seemed to sparkle and shine as gold in the Klondike, and her deep blue eyes were probably like the blues of the ocean that Richie imagined someday seeing. When those eyes glanced over at him, it made him feel uncomfortable, not bad uncomfortable but good, like there was an extra heart beating in his chest or as if a small bird with little wings was trapped in between his ribs and doing its best to escape. Then on one of those walks home that were becoming more frequent, he started to understand what pieces put Tina Price together.

In six years of schooling, she had been in five different schools. Moving from project to project that her father developed must not have been easy, Richie concluded. At least, this was going to be one of this biggest, the development of a golf course and resort on the other side of the hill country and a large outlet mall along the interstate. It would take years to complete. In fact, the construction out along the road past the four corners was the location of their new house, even though they lived in one of the big upscale houses around the corner in the subdivision. Maybe it was all the moving or something else that seemed to occur all too frequently between adults, for her father and mother had separated. When Richie asked how often she saw her mother, he was first answered with a blank stare.

It was on a subsequent long walk home, just as they reached her street and just before she turned away, that Tina blurted out the first words she had not spoken through a smile. On that day, there was a frozen frown on her face as she stated, "My mother is in an institution. She doesn't love us anymore." It would take a long time for Richie to ever even consider approaching the subject again.

The next day and with that smile again on her face, Richie confided something to her—the fact that his father was dead and that he never even had a chance to see him. It seemed only right to tell her, to let her know that others also feel pain. The only way she responded was to say, "Oh, I'm so sorry." But he recognized that she realized he knew how she felt.

Richie's other project was progressing slowly. It was a couple of weeks after they had started that two things occurred. Becka concluded that Tyrone was mildly dyslexic, and that fact sent Richie scurrying to the library to determine what they could do.

That same day, for some strange reason, Richie accumulated the courage to ask Sarah Beamer if she would now start helping him teach that someone to read. And while Tyrone was reluctant, they met that next day after club training, and Richie realized that the two high school students knew each other from associating in certain classes. But it was Sarah who made it work. She erased the embarrassment with an obvious pledge of desiring to help and then sealed the deal with a promise of secrecy. Then there was the soft touch of her hand along Tyrone's arm and a brightness in her eyes when she peered into his face. Somehow when she said, "We can do this, you wait and see," Richie suspected that something special existed between the two of them, something like the feeling he had when he was around Tina.

Now two weeks later and on another Saturday afternoon, Tyrone arrived, driving his great-aunt's car and with books in hand. They had just begun to work when Lady pricked up her ears and a moment later, a car could be heard pulling into the driveway and then the slamming of two doors.

"That must be Sarah, but I wonder who is with her?" Richie stated as he got up to answer the door.

He pulled on the interior door just as Sarah opened what remained of the screen door, and she and the attractive blond-haired woman in jeans and sweatshirt rather than typical school day attire stepped inside.

"Mrs. Learner!" Richie's voice cracked out in surprise. "What are you doing here?"

The exclamation surprised Tyrone, and he shut the book, stood up next to the table, and started putting on his jacket.

"Look, Ty. . .," Sarah said in an explanatory voice and calling him by the nickname that she had personally placed on him. "She has some ideas, some good ideas, and she can help."

Tyrone did not look at Richie or Mrs. Learner, but his stare was at and through Sarah. "How could you? I trusted you. How could you?" His voice quivered.

"Coach's wife"—Tyrone tried to push by his classmate—"what do you think you're doing? I can't have—"

It was Sarah who reacted in a way that Richie thought impossible. There was no longer a smile on her face, and her eyes were wide open and locked on him. She stepped in front of him and violently pulled him around to face her. "Look at me!" she demanded.

Tyrone's face was turned to the door, but Richie was sure that he saw tears in his eyes.

"Look at me, damn it!" Sarah was mean, a thousand times meaner than he Richie had ever seen her in class, and besides, she swore. The opposite of the Sarah he saw in school, Richie thought.

"She is here because I care, I care about you!" She used one of her hands to pull Tyrone's face around.

He swiveled his face back and down in her direction. And with that movement, Sarah Beamer faced him and kissed him. She kissed him not like his mother kissed Richie or the sometime kiss from his great-grandmother that somehow awkwardly would end up on Richie's nose or like the woman contestant kisses Bob Barker when they win the showcase. No, Sarah kissed him fiercely, like the woman kissing a man on the cover of those books in the front rack of the library, the ones that you were not supposed to look at but somehow your eyes seemed to always find.

Sarah looked up at Tyrone, her eyes pouring up into his face. "She knows. She knows we have been dating. I asked her, asked her for help, help with my feelings. I don't want to hide it anymore, Ty. There is nothing wrong with it."

Tyrone tried to push her away, but she wouldn't release her grip. "I'm black, I'm black and stupid. That is a real combination for success, especially with the most beautiful girl in the school. What will the others think?"

"I don't care what they think, and if they think something, that's their problem, not ours." Sarah still poured her gaze up at him.

It was Mrs. Learner who interrupted. "Sarah's right, Ty. If people don't understand, then they are the ones who are the losers. Sarah first came to me because she. . ." Even Mrs. Learner stumbled for words. "She cares about you, you the person, you the human being. Who cares if you are black, white, yellow, or green! She cares enough about you to come to me for help not only with her feelings but because you need help. And when Sarah told me what she did, what Richie and she were doing, well, I think I have some ideas that can help, ideas that we can still keep as our secret."

"Man, this is getting to be way too complicated." Tyrone's voice now contained a tone of frustration. "All I want to do is to be able to read, like Sarah, like Mrs. Small, like Richie, like everyone else."

Somehow, Sarah drew herself even closer to him and wrapped her arms around his chest. "And you will, just trust us."

Tyrone's expression calmed, and he searched the room for the person he trusted most. "What do you think, RJ?" A smile, not the typical wide smile but a smile anyway, appeared on his face.

Richie searched the three faces now starring at him. Even Lady tilted her head as if waiting for an answer. He was befuddled, confused, and bewildered. He looked at Sarah and wondered if there was the feeling of a small bird being trapped in her chest. Richie stammered for certain words and then focused on Mrs. Learner. "I know I can trust her." He pointed toward Mrs. Learner.

That answer was good enough for Tyrone.

They had worked for an hour with Mrs. Learner's ideas when another car door slammed shut out in the driveway, and Becka Small entered with a bag of groceries.

"Hi, Ty, Sarah." Becka nodded in the direction of the newcomer. "Mrs. Learner, what are you doing here?"

"It is a long story, but please, please call me Carol." She was already helping Becka with the bag. "But for now, let us say that I am going to help, if you don't mind."

"Not at all," Becka responded. "But it does seem to be getting a bit crowded in here, and anyway, I know the kids are hungry."

"After working all day, nonsense. How about we order out and send them in to pick it up? Maybe you and I can just sit and talk." Mrs. Learner already had her cell phone to her ear. "Who is in the mood for a couple of pizzas?"

And as Mrs. Learner ordered pizzas, Richie wondered if his mother had ever had that feeling of a small bird being trapped in her chest.

CHAPTER 19

RICHIE HAD NEVER eaten fresh store-purchased pizza. Now he balanced two humungous square boxes by extending his arms as far forward as he possibly could, trying not to let the boxes tilt any other way but toward his upraised chin. It would be a major tragedy of spilled cheese and toppings in the middle of the back seat of Sarah's car if he failed. Tyrone opened the door, and somehow Richie squeezed the still hot boxes through the yawning opening of the car door, onto the seat, and then over to the other side. The fresh smell of the sausage and pepperoni made his mouth water, and his imagination was filled with the thoughts of how this unknown delicacy would taste.

"Having a little trouble there, my man?" Tyrone chuckled as he winked at Sarah and the obvious plight of Richie having to carry the awkward boxes.

Richie didn't care what Tyrone thought. He just wanted to get home in order to enjoy the food, enjoy the succulent taste of all those meat and vegetable toppings swimming around in tomato sauce covering the thick cooked dough curled up liberally at the corners. It didn't sound as delicious when described like that, he thought, but it still admitted a very mouth-watering fragrance. His immediate plans of culinary enjoyment were altered when a big black Mercedes parked perpendicular behind Sarah's car. A distinguished man in a black suit, stark white shirt, and tie exited the vehicle.

"Sarah, good thing I found you." The man seemed hurried. "I have an unexpected meeting that I have to attend, and I promised Mrs. Keeper the night off. Would you be a good girl and sit for me tonight?"

It was obvious that the man did not anticipate being rejected and was already pulling money from a leather wallet. "Mrs. Keeper would like to leave in about fifteen minutes. Would you. . ." For a moment, the man acknowledged the existence of Tyrone and Richie with a simple glance. "Would you stay with her until I get back!" There seemed to be no questioning in his voice.

"Sure, no problem," Sarah said with the typical smile on her face. "In fact, we are just going to have some pizza. I'll pick her up, we'll eat at Richie's place, and I will have her home in an hour."

"Good, Sarah, I know I can depend on you. I'll be home by eleven. I'll pay for those pizzas too." The man handed Sarah money and was immediately back in his car and speeding away.

"Babysitting gig?" Tyrone asked as he got in the car.

"Yep," Sarah responded. "Nice enough man but always in a hurry." She looked at the money in her hand. "I'll drop you two off with the food. Mrs. Learner and your mom are waiting." She turned her head toward Richie and handed him one of the bills.

"Don't want your teacher and your mother talking too much about you when you're not there." Tyrone chuckled. "What's this for?" He turned his attention back to Sarah as she handed him one of the bills.

"Well, he hired *us* to babysit." She accented the word *us*.

"I not any babysitter." Tyrone tried to hand her the money back.

"Tonight you are, at least until after we eat. He asked all of us, and that's your share. Doesn't pay bad either."

Richie looked down at the money in his hand. It was a single bill with the picture of Ulysses S. Grant on it. It was something that he had never seen before, something that even his mother did not have in the jar high up on the shelve where she kept her tips. He was holding a fifty-dollar bill in his hand.

"Who's the kid?" Tyrone inquired.

"You know her, Richie. She's in your class," Sarah commented as she started the vehicle. "That was H.I. Price, you know, Tina's dad."

Richie had fifty dollars in his hand, but it was not the money that made that bird reappear in the middle of his chest and start fluttering its wings. Tina, Tina Price, Sarah was going to bring her back to his house. Tina was coming to the trailer, the old rickety trailer, the outside surrounded by bales of hay to try to keep the cold off the floor, the trailer with the broken porch light, the squeaky front door, old carpeting, and worn furniture. Suddenly, the fluttering in his chest became a churning in his stomach, and the desire for meats and vegetables swimming in tomato sauce had all but disappeared. Richie looked at the money in his hand. There was no amount, he thought, that could pay for the embarrassment he was about to experience.

"I can't take this!" He tried to pass the bill over the seat and alter what he knew was about to happen.

Her smile could be seen through the rearview mirror, a smile that seemed to suggest that she knew that Richie had a crush on a little blond-haired girl in his class. Sure, Richie concluded, she was part-teacher and was developing that ability to look right into your head and read your mind.

"Yes, you can," she responded.

Richie wondered if it was also that obvious to others when you liked someone. Was it something that you could not see but others could, like a pimple coming out on your forehead that everyone else noticed, but until you looked in the mirror you had no idea it had grown to the size of a mountain right over your eyes? It was a surprise to him about Sarah and Tyrone, so maybe it wasn't all that obvious. But Tina was coming to the trailer, and, boy, he thought, was he going to be embarrassed.

CHAPTER 20

I T HAD NOT started off too badly. Becka had set the table with six place settings that Richie did not know even existed. Why would he? he thought. There had typically been only he and his mother at the table. Somehow, napkins appeared that he also never knew existed. The table looked as normal as he could imagine a table appearing. When Sarah arrived with Tina, the table was set, the pizzas kept hot in the oven, and everyone hungry, everyone except Richie.

His mother's immediate call to dinner had hopefully kept the young wide-eyed little blonde from noticing anything more than the table. It is when they sat down that Richie noticed that she smiled at him, grinned at him with a smile that was bigger and better than he had ever seen on any walk home. And then she sat down right next to him at the table and smiled again as if happy to be there. She was a quiet little girl, and Richie liked that because it meant that he was not expected to be involved in conversation. He sat down next to her, and that is when it happened.

Tina reached over and touched him on the arm and left her hand there for a long, breathtaking minute. "I'm so glad that you invited me, Richard. Thank you."

Richie was about to say that he had not invited her and never had any intention of inviting her into the trailer. He would rather have invited Attila the Hun, Dracula, or Ivan the Terrible, even all three infamous characters described in his foray through the encyclopedias. For goodness' sake, he thought, Clarence Goodfellow would be better, even if he didn't leave a crumb for a dog as he vacuumed up the food. It had been nothing more than a hurried man in a black Mercedes that was destroying his first experience with pizza. Then he saw Sarah's beaming smile over the little girl's shoulder and her head nodding yes. He felt the warmth of Tina's hand on his arm, the awful gurgling in his stomach slowly being replaced by the flutter of birds in his rib cage, and then recognized that she had called him Richard, not Richie.

He managed to look back at her and simply said, "You're welcome." Over Tina's shoulder, Sarah nodded her approval and flashed him the big okay sign with her finger and thumb.

They had finished eating. Somehow, the anticipation of pizza had resulted in not being that special, at least not when Tina was around. After dinner, when she asked to see his encyclopedia collection, he was dumbstruck. He didn't even remember telling her about them. But he must have, he concluded, his mind wondering what else he might have unknowingly confided in her.

The two fifth graders positioned themselves on the floor of the living room, Lady between them and conveniently located in order that either of them stroke her across the back of the head and neck. Tina perused Volume G and stopped at Georgia, showing him where she had lived on the map and pointing out some of the topics in the book. Becka, Mrs. Learner and the two high school students sat at the table and talked. Eventually, Tyrone stated he had to get home, and Tina decided to walk Lady with Richie before she and Sarah departed. When they returned, Tyrone was gone and was also taking Mrs. Learner home. Sarah was helping Becka with the dishes.

Tina looked at Richie and posed a question to Sarah. "Sarah, would it be all right if Richard and Lady came over and spent some time at my house tonight?"

"Don't see why not, but it is up to Richie and his mother," she responded. "I can either drop Richie off. . ."

Becka interjected, "How about if I come over and pick him up at ten? That is late enough."

The house was gigantic, like a castle. Why would someone ever desire a bigger one? Richie thought. They stood in an ornate foyer and entryway that fronted a room large enough to hold their entire trailer. The ceiling was at least two stories high. A large fireplace extended across one entire sidewall, and a variety of sofas, chairs, and tables were artfully placed in groupings in the room. Instead of entering, they turned right and into another room that was the library. It seemed to have as many books as the Eureka Springs Public Library, but maybe it was just the fact that books filled every shelf on all of the four walls from floor to ceiling.

"You can borrow any books you want, Richard," Tina offered. "My father doesn't read them because he is too busy. I find many of them very boring."

"What do you two want to do?" Sarah questioned as she entered the room.

"Would you like to watch a movie?" Tina inquired.

Richie just bobbed his head yes.

"Sounds good to me," Sarah said. "How about you two go in and pick out a movie, and I will make us some popcorn."

"Come on, Richard, follow me." Tina motioned Richie toward another door at the opposite end of the room. "You can pick out anything you want."

Richie followed her into a room. One wall was covered by a white screen, a screen at least five times as large as the one that hung above the chalkboard in Mrs. Learner's classroom. He had never seen anything like it, unless he considered the one time he went to a drive-in theater with his mother back in Kentucky. But this was in the house, like a drive-in theater with ten gigantic stuffed chairs facing the screen rather than rows of cars.

"Pick out something you would like to watch," Tina said.

Richie just looked at her.

She went over to several shelves that contained square boxes about the size of books and pulled one of them forward. She smiled at him, that pleasant wonderful smile. "Boys like this kind of stuff." She handed him a box with the first of the *Star Wars* movies in it.

He looked at her dumbfounded and unable to make a decision.

"You'll like it," she said as she turned on the player at the back of the room, took the remote, sat in one of the cushy chairs, dimmed the lights, and started the movie on the screen in front of them by pushing buttons on the remote.

Richie was in awe. He had never seen anything like it. As he started to fall into one of the puffy chairs next to her, the surge of sound rumbled throughout the room and pushed him into the chair as if a gigantic wave had rolled over him. With a blaze of light and blaring of music, the movie started. And while he did not feel too at home, Lady sat down on the floor between them, rested her head on her paws, stretched out, and, amidst the glare and noise, closed her eyes.

The sound engulfed the entire room, and Richie sat wide-eyed as the picture began in a bold brilliance that the old television set at his home could never have imagined. It was like he was there in space, looking at space fighters and distant stars, almost as one of them. He did not notice when Lady raised her head and turned it from side to side and then stood with the fur on the back of her head bristling upward. It was only when she bound from the room and growled that Richie noticed. He rose and started to follow.

As he left the room, he heard the vicious barking of the dog, the breaking of what he thought to be glass, and then the scream from Sarah. He ran toward the noise, toward the kitchen somewhere in the back of the house. When he finally wound his way through the hallways and rooms and to the kitchen, Sarah was cowering near the refrigerator and away from the outside wall, her stare going out through the partially open sliding patio door. Glass from the shattered window lay scattered over the kitchen floor, along with a broken glass bowl that Sarah probably had dropped. Out over the patio and somewhere out in the expansive yard, Lady could be heard viciously barking.

"Where is Tina?" Sarah asked in panic. "Someone was in the house, here in the house."

"Here I am, Sarah." The little girl entered the kitchen and was immediately swooped up next to the teenager.

It was Richie who took charge. He grabbed the telephone from the wall and dialed 911 just as they had talked about at school. He spoke forcefully. "We need a policeman. Someone has broken in to the house." He answered the operator's questions calmly and specifically but was still unsure of what they should do. Maybe go to a neighbor like the operator was suggesting, he thought.

"No." He told the operator. "You stay on the line until the police get here. We'll be okay." Richie knew they would because through the black of the darkening night he saw Lady crossing the patio with part of a man's pant leg draped from her mouth.

CHAPTER 21

THE BEAM OF Sergeant Learner's flashlight pierced the dark night over the corn stubble in the farm field behind the Price house. "Richie, I want you to stay right with me at all times." He recognized that Lady would do nothing unless Richie commanded.

"Yes, sir," Richie responded.

Tina and Sarah were both back with Becka at the trailer with Constable Friendly of the Eureka Springs Police Department posted in a car outside. Somehow, Learner did not buy the fact that the intruder was a burglar whom they had surprised. Nothing appeared out of place at the house, and to Learner, it appeared that the man lay in wait for someone coming home. Tina's father had been contacted and was on his way back from Traverse City, and until he returned, Tina would stay with Becka.

Richie opened the plastic bag and allowed Lady to sniff the torn part of the pant leg and then pointed in the direction of where a single footstep could be seen entering the thawing cornfield. Without hesitation, Lady was off. Even over the half-frozen ground and without a trace of light, the dog moved forward quickly out into the field. She stopped momentarily at a spot where some corn stubble had been beaten down and where someone had stopped. The beam of Sergeant Learner's flashlight exposed fresh blood scattered on the corn stubble and the ground. Then the dog turned and moved away from the house and deeper into the field. The path zigzagged through the field, crossed a still partially frozen ditch, and then headed due west for a mile until it intersected a dirt road. The dog followed the trail along the shoulder of the road for about three hundred yards, stopped, lifted her head from the ground, and turned it upward.

Both Richie and Sergeant Learner were out of breath as they approached the now stopped dog. She turned and looked at Richie and Sergeant Learner next to him. There in the road was the tire track of one wheel from a vehicle that had broken through a puddle covered with ice and traveled out to Cumberland to the south. Next to the track were four cigarette butts. The police office took rubber gloves from one of his pockets and started to examine one of the still smoldering cigarettes. Several were still warm. He placed all of them into a plastic envelope he had also extracted from his pocket and then called on his handheld radio for assistance from another state trooper and waited for the car to arrive.

He looked down the road where Lady still stood and also gazed in the direction of the paved road five hundred yards away. The dog turned her head back toward him and gave out a short snort as if clearing the complex airway in her snout. It was obvious to both the dog and the police officer that there was something more going on than a botched burglary.

Mr. Price's black Mercedes pulled up onto the dirt driveway in front of the trailer. Constable Friendly got out of the car to meet him. He could explain nothing to Mr. Price as he rushed toward the front door of the trailer and, without knocking, through the door.

"Where is my daughter?" he demanded in a harsh voice as both Sarah and Becka rose from the sofa to meet him.

Becka tried to calm him. "She is finally asleep in Richie's room and is welcome to stay until morning, Mr. Price."

"In a place like this!" Price looked around the trailer. "I'd think she would be much better off with me than a dump like this."

Becka did not feel angry, she felt ashamed, ashamed that someone would refer to her home in such a manner. She worked hard to keep it clean, to keep it as their home for her and her son. And while it might not be much, it was all the two of them had.

Even though she was small, she did not like being pushed around. "No matter what you think about this place, she is finally asleep, warm and comfortable. It might just be best that she stay until morning. This will not be so frightening to her in the daylight."

"Look, do not tell me what is best for my child," he responded.

Just as he finished, Lady, Richie, and Sergeant Learner entered. The dog looked at the newcomer, decided to ignore him, pushed open the door, and trotted into Richie's bedroom. Learner introduced himself to Price and filled him in on the details that he had so far. Price listened impatiently and reiterated his desire to get his daughter.

"Is she in there with that dog?"

Richie moved toward his bedroom as Price pushed on by him, entered, and flipped on the light. Tina lay on the bed with Lady lying next to her, her arm curled around the dog's neck.

"Daddy, I'm scared." The little girl's faint voice echoed through the room.

"It will be all right, darling." The man spoke affectionately. "Let's go home."

The girl nodded her head no. "I want to stay here with Lady." The dog perked up her ears at the sound of her name and nudged the side of the girl's face with her snout.

Her father seated himself on the bed and tried to hug her daughter still clutching the dog's neck. "Is this the dog that chased away the burglar?" Price stroked the dog's head.

No one immediately responded, and Price started picking up his daughter. "How much do you want for the dog?" He turned to Becka.

"She is not for sale, Mr. Price. That is my son's dog."

"Everything is for sale, madam," Price said snidely. "I'll write you a check for a thousand dollars." He saw Becka not even flinch at the mention of money. "Five thousand then," he continued.

Becka, the small diminutive woman, stared back at him. In a firm loud voice that seemed so opposite of her size, she spoke. "Mr. Price, there are certain things that money cannot buy. I may live in a dump, as you describe it, but it is a home for my son, his dog, and me. We are a family, the three of us, and while money may be able to buy you anything you want, it will never become more important to us than each other."

Becka moved to the side of the door. "I suggest that you take your daughter and leave. Obviously, you listen to no one and care about nothing other than what money can buy." She seemed taller and stronger the more she spoke. "And I feel sorry for you because no matter how much money you have, you are very poor, Mr. Price, very poor."

Two days later, after Tina Price had arrived home from school, a man and a woman came to the Price house to supposedly repair the telephone. Mrs. Keeper had even noticed that the telephone line had gone dead about twenty minutes earlier. Dressed in work shirts like telephone repair personnel and driving a white van, Mrs. Keeper admitted them to the house. Who would have expected a man and a woman? One hour later, she was able to work the tape from around one of her wrists, untie her other hand, and run to the neighbors to call the police. Tina Price had been kidnapped.

CHAPTER 22

TWO AGONIZING DAYS had passed. The Federal Bureau of Investigation had taken over the search, and the Michigan State Police had been relegated to performing services as directed by the bureau. Mostly that meant filling the coffeepots and getting the doughnuts. And as far as the investigation, there had been no developments. There was no ransom note or contact from the kidnappers, and the entire village of Eureka Springs held its collective breath in anticipation of news, hopefully good.

On the third day after the abduction, winter continued to release its grip on the upper part of mid-Michigan. The warmth of the sun in a clear blue sky helped defrost the ground while the huge piles of snow in parking lots and along the edge of the roads quickly were shrinking into pools of water. Somehow, signs of spring lifted the spirits of the searchers even without any headway being made. Today, Richie found himself running to the edge of town where the agents had established a command post in the township hall. He, like the others in town, was desperate for any news. Richie had seldom visited the far side of the small town, but as they did, Lady and he would run past the store owned by Frank Savage. As they neared, Lady slowed, sniffed the air, and suddenly went into a frenzy, barking and growling in front of the store owned by the man who had struck Becka months earlier.

It was strange, Richie thought, that Lady would still display anger after so many months. As they came to the edge of the store, Lady unexpectedly turned and ran down the sidewall and toward the back of the building. The store was closed, like many of the stores in Eureka Springs, the owners and employees volunteering for the teams that were unsuccessfully searching the countryside under the watchful eye of the FBI. Still, Lady faced the rear door of the building, the fur on her back bristling upward while accompanied by a low mean growl. Even with Richie's demands, the dog would not leave the door, and finally, Richie pulled her away by grabbing the hair on her neck.

"What's gotten into you, Lady?" Richie talked to the dog as if she could understand. "We have more problems than worrying about Mr. Savage. Come, girl." Richie tugged and finally pulled the dog away.

They had arrived at the township hall where an array of police vehicles was haphazardly scattered across the parking lot. Richie walked among the cars hoping, as he did on the previous day, to overhear some news. Finally, after being amidst the vehicles and the various officers coming and going for the better part of an hour, he was able to sneak into the building, as some officers left the door swinging open when they departed. He wandered about trying not to look too suspicious and then turned to find Lady. There in front of him stood Frank Savage with the dog eyeing him carefully.

"Hey, kid"—he looked at Richie—"I'm not too sure about you being in here, especially with her." He carefully eyed the dog while making no sudden movements and cordially speaking to Richie.

"Frank, do you think you have more cable at your store? We would like to run some more radio equipment over to the desks." The request came from a man wearing a blue windbreaker with the letters "FBI" scrawled across the back.

"Already in the back of my truck, be there in a minute," Savage responded before shifting his attention back to Richie. "Kid, it might be best that you and your dog not be in here." There was forced expression of pleasantness on his face as he suspiciously eyed the dog and then turned and joined the agent making the request.

Lady snorted an unimposing grunt in the direction of Savage and returned to her master's side.

Richie and Lady departed the building and retraced their footsteps back through town. Again, as they passed the building where Mr. Savage ran his business, but this time on the opposite side of the street, Lady went into a rage and started to cross the road. Only a firm lock of his hands intertwined in her fur stopped Lady at the curb. Yet it was strange, Richie thought, because Lady had come in direct contact with Frank Savage at the township hall and hardly even reacted. Yet when she passed the store, she became almost uncontrollable. Something was wrong, Richie concluded, but what was it? Obviously, Frank Savage had nothing to do with Tina's disappearance because he was assisting the police. He could go back to the command post and tell them about how Lady reacted, but Frank Savage was there helping. No, Richie decided, the best one to tell, the one who would understand would be Coach Learner. As Lady and he were passing through the not-so-sprawling downtown area of Eureka Springs, a car pulled up next to them.

"Hey, RJ, is there any news?" Big Ben Shoulders was speaking through the side window of the car driven by Tyrone.

Richie shook his head no as he and Lady approached the vehicle. "But I have to find Coach Learner. Do either of you know where he is at?"

"Maybe the school," Ben responded. "Or out on one of the search parties. We tried to volunteer, but right now they have enough searchers."

"Hop in," Ty stated. "Let's drive over to the school and see if his car is there."

After Richie and Lady got in the back seat, he explained what had happened at the store and then his encounter with Frank Savage. As he did so, Ty made a U-turn and headed in the direction they had come.

"What you doing, Ty?" Ben questioned.

"There is something in that store," Ty responded.

"Well then, let's go tell the FBI about it," Ben said.

"Tell them what, that a dog barks at a back door? And besides, maybe this Savage guy is involved. How do we get by him and talk with someone without him becoming suspicious?" Ty had already pulled up and around to the back side of the building. "Besides, we're here. Let's see what we can find."

Lady was first out of the car and went directly to the rear door of the building. Somehow, she understood that they would be going in and seemed to ready herself as if she would be searching for something. Ben watched down the side of the building as Ty tried turning the doorknob and pushing on the door. Not only did the doorknob not turn but two other faceplates of deadbolts were visible above and below the knob.

"Getting in isn't going to be easy," Ty whispered.

"Let me take a look." Ben moved toward the door, looked at the three locks, drew in a deep breath, pulled back slightly from the opening, and then slammed his broad shoulder into the door next to the frame. There was the sharp crackle of splintering wood as the door swung open, all three bolts of the locks being pushed through the sturdy but now shredded frame.

"Didn't take much at all," Ty stated as he looked at the splintered casing and back at Ben. "So much for locks."

It was Lady who reacted first. She was instantaneously through the door, and Richie recognized that she was on the scent of something. Immediately, she was pawing at a rubber garbage can with a lid securely snapped on top. Ty pulled off the lid and was suddenly greeted with the stench of rotting garbage.

"No sense being timid," Ty stated as he spilled the contents on the ground. "It's not like no one will know we were here."

Blackening vegetables and half-eaten food spilled onto the floor. Lady glanced at the mess on the floor and went right back to the plastic container. She began to paw at the rubber sides.

"That's it, nothing else." Ben looked down into the black plastic bag that still served as a liner. "Nothing, empty, see?" He spoke toward Lady as he pulled the black bag from the container. But Lady would not give up, she tipped over the garbage can, ran her head inside, and pulled out still another plastic bag that had been squashed flat in the very bottom.

Ty was the first to grab it from her mouth, untie the knot in the top, and spill out the contents. There on the floor was a pair of men's trousers, part of one pant leg having been ripped off just below the knee and what appeared to be dried blood on the tattered fabric.

Richie looked at Ty and Ben, and then they all stared down at the pants on the floor. Ben picked up the garment and carefully placed it back in the bag.

"Was Savage limping?" Ty asked Richie.

"I don't think so, and anyway, Lady paid him no attention," Richie answered

"There must be something else around here. Let's take a look around." Ben suggested.

The three of them rummaged through items scattered around the room that acted as a storage area for the store. Nothing seemed unusual until Ty picked up a large cylindrical tube, pulled off the lid, and unrolled a map. It was an old map that seemed to show the location of hills with lines snaking over and around the mounds.

Richie looked at the legend and read the words out loud. "Blackmore Coal Company 1902." Ben and Ty looked at him as he continued, "It's a topographical map of the mines over in the hill country."

"Maybe, maybe that is where they are hiding Tina," Ben stated. "But it is a pretty big area, those mines run for miles." Ben pointed at the designation for distance on the legend of the map.

Richie looked down at Lady. "Not if we have Lady. All we need now is some of Tina's clothing, a jacket or something. Gee, I have her scarf at home, but it has been washed too many times."

"Well, let's go get something else," Ty responded. "You know where she lives. And if Coach Learner's car isn't at the school, we'll call him from the house. He'll know what to do."

CHAPTER 23

COACH LEARNER'S CAR was not at the school, but Carl Leader was, and now the four of them and Lady stood in front of the Price residence. No one was home.

"What do we do now?" Ben asked.

"Well, we broke into the store, why not this house?" Ty stated.

Ty looked out and around the neighborhood and then started them toward the back of the house. "Come on, let's make this quick. We don't need any more attention."

But it was too late. Clarence Goodfellow had seen them and turned his bicycle up the driveway. He pulled on the hand brakes and stopped, at least, the bike did as his torso continued to slowly jiggle to its final resting place.

"No one is home. I saw Mrs. Keeper leave about thirty minutes ago." He eyed them suspiciously. "Hey, what are you guys up to away?"

It was Richie who saw an opportunity. "Clarence, we need your help."

"Sure, Smallie," Clarence responded snidely. "Anything for the tiniest—"

Richie cut off his statement. "Look, Clarence, we don't need your crap right now, just your help. It's important, or we wouldn't be here." He spoke with authority, and it surprised Clarence and the others.

Leader eyed Goodfellow with suspicion. "Can he be trusted?" He voiced the statement to Richie but loud enough for Clarence to hear.

"Yeah, he can be a help. He is a pretty good guy." Richie was surprised by the way he responded and faced Clarence. "We think we know where they have Tina, and we need a piece of her clothing, something for Lady to use in order to track her."

"Well, why didn't you say so?" Clarence hustled over to the lamp next to the garage door, unscrewed the bottom faceplate, and produced a key. "That is how Tina gets in if no one is home."

"Hey, thanks." Tyrone slapped Clarence on the back.

All five of them now stood inside the Price residence but with Richie holding Tina's jacket and with Clarence being filled in as to what was going on.

"We still have to get in touch with Coach," Ben said. "Maybe we call the FBI and tell them what we know."

"Too risky, what if that Savage guy overhears it? I think he is involved," Ty stated. "Look up the Learner home telephone number."

Richie quickly pawed through the telephone book, found the number, and dialed. Someone who identified herself as Carol Learner's sister answered and informed them that her sister and brother-in-law would be returning within the hour.

"Please have Coach Learner wait at home, it's important. Tell him that we have some information about Tina. Tell him Richie, Tyrone, Carl, and Ben called. He'll know who we are." Richie looked around the room and then continued, "Clarence, Clarence Goodfellow, is coming over. Have Coach Learner wait there for Clarence if he gets home first."

Richie turned to his old nemesis. "Clarence, we need you to go to this address." Richie jotted down the number and street on a piece of paper as he finished explaining to Clarence what was happening. "Then you tell Coach Learner about what we found. We are taking Lady up to the old Blackmore Coal Mines and see if we can find Tina."

"And don't forget, I think this Savage guy is involved," Tyrone added. "We can't let him find out."

"You got that, Clarence?" Richie asked as they all filed out of the house and piled into the car.

"Yeah," Clarence responded as they got on his bike and started down the driveway. "And, Richie"—he looked over his shoulder as he turned into the street—"thanks for letting me help."

Clarence was waiting at the residence when the Learners arrived home forty-five minutes later.

Frank Savage had left the township hall feeling potentially a lot richer. Few knew that a ransom note had been received, payment had been arranged, and funds had been transferred to a bank account in a foreign country within hours. Two million dollars split three ways was not a bad take for an easy kidnapping, he smiled as he thought about the number. And with him assisting in the installation of the communications system at the township hall, the upcoming communications failure made their escape that much simpler.

He pulled up to the back of his store. As he parked, he looked over and saw the splintered casing around the rear door of his store. Quickly entering, he was greeted by the stench of the spilled garbage and the realization that the bag containing his cousin's trousers was gone. There was the empty tube on the worktable that had contained the layout of the Blackmore Mines, and there were also the footprints left by a dog that had trotted through the soupy mess left on the floor.

"That damn kid and the dog again!" he cussed angrily in an almost whisper as he reached up and along the wood slat above the door and found the six-shot revolver, jammed it in his pocket, and ran to his car.

There was still plenty of time to warn his cousin and his cousin's wife and get out of the state and then the country and start enjoying the money, he concluded. He had been able to feed the FBI enough false information to have them looking in the opposite direction and concentrating their efforts in chasing after the ransom money that would soon be out of their reach. He could quickly drive out to where they were hiding the girl, and they could escape up through Michigan and then into Canada. They could leave the girl in the complex of mines. If they found her, fine, and who cared what happened to the girl anyway. But if he could ever find that dog, it would be a different story.

CHAPTER 24

AFTER THEY HAD arrived in the hill country, it had taken forty-five minutes for Lady to find a trail that might lead to Tina. As they traversed another grouping of small hills, the scream of a girl could be heard in the distance. Breaking into a run over the crest of the next rise, a man and a woman could be seen in a small clearing standing over broken planking that covered an abandoned shaft.

Lady did not wait and instantaneously raced forward and attacked the man. As he attempted to limp back to a small cabin, the dog drove him to the ground and tore into bandages that wrapped his one leg. The man screamed for help as Richie ordered the dog off him, and Ben simply picked him up and slammed him into an awkward seated position against the face of a rock wall. Carl and Tyrone pulled the woman away from the hole.

"We heard this girl scream." The woman tried to explain away any involvement in the kidnapping. "Is this the little girl everyone is looking for?"

Carl pushed her in Ben's direction. "Sit her down next to the guy. Make sure they don't move." He spoke gruffly.

Richie and Tyrone carefully pulled the loose planking away from the hole and peered down into the darkness. A whimper and then a soft moan could be heard.

"She's down there!" There was a panic in Richie's voice.

"Ty, see if there is a flashlight or lantern in the cabin," Carl ordered.

Ty was back in a moment with both. Taking the flashlight, Carl leaned over, placed his hand on the opposite side of the shaft, and directed the light toward the bottom. The shaft narrowed about eight feet below ground level and then twisted slightly to the right. But there at the bottom of the pit lying in a pool of water, they could see the legs of Tina Price in the beam of light.

"I can get down there," Richie stated emphatically.

"How?" Carl asked and then turned back to Tyrone. "Was there any rope in the cabin?"

"She might be drowning. I can shimmy down the sidewalls."

Before Carl could stop him, Richie had dropped down into the shaft and, by pressing against the walls with his hands, lowered himself down to the bend. He found a foothold on an edge created by the curve, and Carl dropped him the flashlight. Tucking the flashlight into the front of his trousers, he curled around the bend and used his hands, elbows, and knees to shimmy farther down. Suddenly, the shaft widened, and he was forced to drop the last six feet to the bottom.

With the aid of the flashlight, Richie could see that she was bleeding from a wicked-looking gash over her right eye. He knew better than to move her but determined that she was breathing and awake. Slowly, she focused her eyes on him, the blood still oozing from the head wound. He took off his parka and placed it on top of her. Then tearing off a piece of his shirt sleeve, he folded it into a compress and pressed it against the cut on her head.

Carl peered down, trying to see what Richie was doing. "Is she all right?" he screamed out to Richie just as Lady turned and leaped at the man approaching through the woods.

Amazingly, there was no panic in Richie's voice. "She is breathing. Her eyes are open, but she is bleeding from a cut over her eye. There is a lot of blood." He knew what to do. He had read about first aid in the F volume of the encyclopedia.

Then there was the sudden and unexpected blast from a pistol. One shot and then a second as Lady was leaping out and onto the approaching Frank Savage. Savage stumbled backward, the dog still latched onto his upper arm with her jaws. With a loud grunt, Savage sprawled out on the hard rocky surface.

Tyrone was the first to react. Dropping the rope he had found in the cabin and seeing the revolver spin off to the side, he scrambled over and grabbed the weapon. "Stay down, mister, or I'll shoot!" Tyrone hollered as Savage pushed the dog off him.

"You don't want to shoot me, kid," Savage said. "Besides, I'm here to help. I'm working with the police." He attempted to get to his feet, Lady now in a limp mass next to him.

"Look, kid, give me the gun before someone gets hurt." Savage moved closer to Tyrone.

"Mister, I mean it!" Tyrone held the weapon out in his direction while moving back a step and then another. Suddenly, his heels caught on a rocky edge, and he stumbled backward, a third round going off harmlessly in the air but with the gun again falling on the ground between the two of them.

Savage was quick to react and scurried forward to retrieve the weapon. But as he took a second step, a forearm knocked him to the ground with an echoing thud. Coach Learner drove another forearm into his chin and then viciously twisted him over by yanking on his arm as he ran his hands through a set of handcuffs. A moment later, the out-of-breath Clarence Goodfellow appeared.

Learner reached out and picked up the weapon. "Where is Richie?"

"In the mine shaft, Coach, with Tina," Carl answered.

Learner knelt over the shaft and pointed his own flashlight toward the bottom some thirty feet below. "Richie, whatever you do, don't try to move her, at least not yet. Stay calm, more help is on the way."

Quickly, Learner assessed the situation. There was no way that anyone his size or the size of the other players could shimmy down the shaft. "Richie, is there another way out?"

Slowly, Richie scanned the walls of the cavern with the flashlight. Two smaller shafts ran into the pit from different directions. "There are some other openings, Coach, but they are even smaller than the one I came down."

Richie moved over so he could be seen in the light from the state trooper's flashlight and slowly and calmly spoke up at them. "There is no way I can get her up through here by myself."

He pointed upward in the shaft. "But I think. . ." He hesitated as he examined the narrowing space above him. "I think if we fashion something like a harness, I can help guide her up, and we can pull her out."

He moved farther into view and tried not to shout. "I have the bleeding stopped." He cupped his hands and tried to speak quietly. "No broken bones." He looked back in her direction. "Maybe a…" He stopped and pointed to his left forearm and used his other hand to twist on it, indicating to them that her arm might be broken.

"Find me two pieces of wood, maybe ten inches long." Richie still tried to focus his voice upward and away from Tina. "Something for a splint."

Learner leaned back from the hole as other state police troopers and FBI Agents scrambled over the hill and into the clearing. Amazing, he thought, he had a small injured girl trapped in a well, and he was being told what to do by a fifth grader, a fifth-grade boy whom he had chosen because of his heart.

"Where is the girl?" the lead FBI agent demanded. "I'll be taking over here," he continued.

"No, I'm in charge here!" Learner had been bossed around enough by the FBI and defiantly stood and faced the tall lanky agent. "And besides, I already have a man down there with the girl."

Carl tried to hand Coach the ten-inch pieces of wood. "Drop them down to Richard," he said calmly as he spoke in the agent's face. "There are elastic bandages in the first aid kit that Trooper Danielson has, and we can start fashioning a sling with the rope." He turned away from the agent and back toward what he had been doing.

Not willing to take on Learner, the agent turned toward Carl, Ben, and Tyrone. "Who's down there with the girl?"

All three looked back at the agent. "Richard Small. He is one of us," they said simultaneously.

Fifteen minutes later, a blond-haired girl with a bandage made from a part of a boy's shirt and holding a compress in place on her head, her arm in a splint made of two wood pieces and elastic bandages and her body wrapped in the blue parka with the word *Panthers* scrawled across the front appeared from the narrow shaft having been carefully guided upward, around the bend, and to the surface in a sort of body harness.

Then the person whom Coach Learner had described as a man climbed the rope and was pulled from the mouth of the narrow well. In front of a several dozen FBI agents, state troopers, and rescue personnel stood a fifth-grade boy. He was dirt-covered, his forearms scrapped raw from the climb down, the tips of several fingers cut and bleeding, and the knees of his only other pair of pants shredded away and showing his skinned knees. He stood there bare-chested, his shirt used for bandages and his parka to warm the girl. In the cool air, the perspiration from his body formed a warm vapor that rose off his shoulders. One lens of his glasses displayed a single long crack, and he pushed them up and firmly back onto his nose. No one saw a boy. No one saw a small boy with broken black-framed thick glasses. Each one of them knew they were looking at a hero.

"Where is Lady?" Richie looked around and through the people who had started to pat him on his shoulder. A trooper took off his jacket and draped it over his back. "Where is Lady?" he asked again.

The sea of people parted. Another state trooper was kneeling over the dog. Clarence Goodfellow, big blubbery Clarence Goodfellow, sat on the ground. In his lap rested the head of a dog, her eyes glazed and her head barely able to swivel in Richie's direction.

The trooper looked over at Learner. "Savage shot her." He was shaking his head no as he spoke.

Clarence looked up at Richie, and through the flood of tears that flushed over his round cheeks down onto his double and triple chin, he looked up and spoke. "Richie, she's dying. Lady is dying."

CHAPTER 25

L ADY DIED THE next morning. Assisted by two veterinarians from Michigan State University and flown up to Eureka Springs by the state police, Dr. Wild had done his best to save the life of the badly injured animal. Becka, Coach Learner and his wife, Clarence Goodfellow, Tyrone, Carl Leader, and Ben Shoulders had waited the entire evening with Richie in the offices of Dr. Wild. Now in the light of morning, others from the village had begun to gather outside the offices.

Since Richie had refused to go to the emergency clinic in Mancelona, Dr. Achers had come to the offices and cleaned and bandaged the numerous cuts and scrapes on Richie's fingers, hands, arms, and knees. Around eight thirty in the morning, Dr. Wild came out and tried to console Richie but found a boy, his hands wrapped in bandages and as stoic in his demeanor as a person could be. There was no crying, no tears, just the sad expression of loss in eyes that penetrated into everyone whom he happened to gaze at.

At nine o'clock, Dr. Wild handed over the body of a sixty-five-pound dog bundled in a light blue blanket to the boy whom she had grown to love. He would bury what was left behind the trailer he called home.

"Richard, why don't we put her in the back of the patrol car?" Sergeant Learner offered. "I will drive you home."

"No, sir, I would like to carry her." Richie peered up at Coach Learner. "We ran this way on many days. At least, I can carry her home one more time."

"But it's three miles, Richie," Becka exclaimed.

"Its okay, Mom. I'd like to walk." And with the statement, Tyrone opened the door for a young man, his hands in bandages and his scraped knees showing through his torn pants as he carried the dog he had come to love.

Tyrone, Carl, Ben, and Clarence fell in around him, and they departed the office and started down Main Street and through town. Others from the club were the first to join and then students, businesspeople from the stores in town, anyone who knew what happened, and it became a quiet procession of a dozen, then several dozen, then a hundred, and then more than a hundred following a young man carrying the body of his dog.

The weight of the animal was almost two-thirds of Richie's own weight, but he continued down the street and up the hill, still carrying the body, never flinching but his arms straining with the weight.

"RJ, let me help," Tyrone stated.

Reluctantly, Richie acquiesced and allowed his friend to carry the body for less than an eighth of a mile while sensation returned to his arms. Carl and Ben took turns carrying the blue bundle but with Richie bearing the weight of the body for the majority of the route. Finally, as they approached Cumberland, Clarence asked if he could carry her. Richie placed the body in the big boy's arms, and with gigantic tears running down and around his face, he carried the dog to the corner.

People followed, some walking, others now joining the procession in their vehicles in a long slow-moving line. They turned onto the gravel driveway, went around the trailer, and stood in the backyard as Richie knelt and placed the dog on the ground. Then on a small natural mound at the edge of the cut cornfield, Richie knelt and started digging and pawing with his bandaged hands in the thawing dirt of spring.

Ben and Tyrone knelt next to him, each grasping a hand as Richie just stared at the impression he had started in the ground. It was Sid Glum, dressed in a pair of jeans and a sweatshirt and looking nothing like the principal, who produced a shovel.

He patted Richie on the back as he knelt. "Richard, may I be the first to help?" His statement was in the form of the most questioning of questions, and the three boys moved away as the principal took the first three bites out of the black soil.

Coach Learner went next, then Tyrone, Ben, and Carl, and then others from the team, each digging the grave a little deeper. Clarence stood in the hole up to his thighs and threw out several shovels of dirt. Then Assistant Principal Bad, Mr. Reid, the librarian's husband, Dr. Wild, and Mrs. Driver's husband all took their turns.

Finally, Richie took the shovel and dropped down into the pit now as deep as his chin. He threw out shovel after shovel until his head could barely be seen in the hole. With the cuts on his hands reopened and blood accumulating in the bandages, he pulled himself out, took the blanket off the body, and started to lift what remained of the dog. Tyrone and Coach Learner jumped in the pit and accepted the broken body of the animal and set it in the grave.

The dirt Richie shoveled back in echoed up from the deep hole. Then Tyrone took the shovel and continued and then Coach Learner, Carl, Ben and countless others. As the final bit of soil was mounded up onto the grave, Richie turned to his mother.

His eyes were open and wide, and he spoke in a clear calm voice heard by all those around him. "Why? Why, Mom, did Lady have to die?"

Becka pulled him close to her. He was bigger, taller than just five months ago, and it suddenly became obvious to her. "Because she loved you, would do anything for you. She died protecting you, Tina, and the others."

As Richie's head rested alongside his mother's, for the first time, tears started to silently flush through the dirt on his face. Streaks appeared on his cheeks, and then the flood of emotion washed his face almost clean. He felt humiliated to cry in front of the others, but there was no need to be embarrassed because a hundred others were sobbing even more.

———

Dr. Jennifer Cares had worked feverishly on the dying animal. She and her partner, Dr. John Canine, were two of the best animal trauma doctors in the state, maybe the country, both flown up from Michigan State by the state police. One bullet had severed the spine near the hips, and the other had torn savagely through the chest cavity. They would have put her down hours earlier, but the dog wanted to survive long enough to birth the six premature puppies that still lay inside her.

They were vehement at giving the puppies a chance, a chance for survival, but it was a long shot. But still, the mother remained alive knowing that she could still give them that chance.

"Does anyone realize that the dog was even pregnant?" Jennifer asked Dr. Wild.

"I don't think so. They are so undeveloped, weeks early. I don't think anyone realized."

Lady tried to turn her head as the last tiny-as-a-thumb puppy spilled out of the incision made by Dr. Canine. Four males and two females all probably destined to die, but as the last was delivered, Lady laid her head back down on the table for the very last time and lay perfectly still.

"Should we tell the boy?" Jennifer asked.

"And break his heart a second time when they are gone too?" Dr. Wild answered. "They really don't stand a chance, this little, this premature."

But Jennifer refocused her attention on the tiny newborns. One of the males was born dead, and another succumbed shortly after Richie and the others left the office. There were four left, breathing, warm, but soon to starve in the toasty incubator unless she found some way to consistently feed them. It was then that Lioness, the pet cat in Dr. Wild's office, carefully wandered over and stood next to the closed incubator. Her kittens of six weeks had just been weaned, and now she just stared through the glass at the huddled little mass of hairless pups.

Jennifer opened the lid. Lioness looked over at her playful kittens and then back into the incubator. Without hesitation, she deftly leaped into the box, carefully positioned herself around the struggling creatures, and pushed them upward to her warm stomach with the top of her leg. Slowly, the still blind pups instinctively sought out the warmth of her belly and started suckling the milk she could still provide.

While Dr. Canine returned to East Lansing, Jennifer, along with Dr. Wild, made it their mission to try and save the remaining puppies. The next day, one of the females succumbed, and Jennifer sadly separated the tiny body from the remaining three. Later that afternoon, the remaining female seemed to struggle, but it was Lioness who nudged her back to life and assured that the small mouth found a nipple for more milk. Jennifer and Dr. Wild did everything medically possible to increase their chances, taking shifts watching the animals, cleaning them, and making sure they were warm and being fed. It would be a struggle, an almost impossible struggle, but both knew that there was a little boy out there who was coping with his own loss.

CHAPTER 26

BECKA SMALL SWIVELED away from the order window, three entrees extending down her arm from somewhere above her elbow and another balanced in her other hand. It was easier to carry than to use a tray, especially when the two other waitresses had called in sick, and now she was the hostess, only waitress, and cashier during the end of a busy afternoon shift.

"Be with you in a moment," she said to the two men who had entered the door to Fred Feeder's Diner.

She delivered the entrees to the table of two couples, somehow grabbed a coffeepot, and replenished drinks at another. She was immediately clearing off the table so the two men could be seated, directing them in that direction, and then cashed out a party of three at the register, always with a pleasant smile on her face.

Mr. Price had entered several moments earlier and crossed over to Sam Planner, his architect for mall construction, sitting in a booth near the back. In another minute, she was at their table.

"Yes, gentlemen, didn't see you come in." She apologized. "May I start you off with something to drink?" She first made eye contact with her customers, and the smile diminished on her face. "Something to drink, Mr. Price?"

"Look, I would like to start with an apology." He spoke sincerely. "I really was a jerk, and I had no right to act like that. I am truly sorry." He hesitated. "But I would like to talk to you, if it is all right."

"Mr. Price, I am at the end of a very busy lunch hour. I just don't have the time, and anyway, I accept the apology."

"It's very important." Price was insistent.

"Well, in about thirty minutes, this place will be close to empty. If you want to wait, that is up to you." She still had a questioning look on her face.

"Yes, coffee, please." He responded while also pointing to the other man. She seemed to be gone for only the slightest moment, returned to pour each of them a cup, provided them a menu, and recited the day's specials.

"Just coffee for now," he stated.

She turned and walked away while refilling coffee cups and then took the order of the men who had just arrived.

"What do you think, Sam?" Mr. Price asked of his longtime employee who was also in charge of restaurant setups at numerous malls around the country.

"Well, I will say one thing. She is one of the most hard-working waitresses I have ever seen. Fast, efficient, courteous, and handles the customers in a manner that leaves all of them happy." Planner explained.

It had been almost two weeks since Lady was buried. Price had tried to contact Becka Small, thank her for what Richie and Lady had done, but she had no phone, and the letters were returned unaccepted. He had discovered that she had returned anything anyone offered in rewarding Richie, anything but a free eye examination for her son and two new pair of glasses. She was a proud woman, a self-sufficient woman, and he respected that more than most knew.

Sam and Mr. Price watched for the next thirty minutes as she ran the entire restaurant other than the kitchen with choreographed perfection. Finally, as the restaurant was emptying, she returned to pour them still another cup of coffee.

"Ms. Small, we'd like to talk to you. May I call you Rebecca?" Planner asked.

"I prefer Becka," she responded. "Talk to me about what?"

"Well, Mr. Price, as you may know, is involved in the construction of the new mall back up the interstate and the resort over on the other side of the hills."

She looked at Planner and then at Price. "How does that involve me?"

"He is going to construct several restaurants in conjunction with the project. Do you have any fine dining experience?" Planner asked.

A pleasant smile crossed her face. "Do you mean that Friendly Fred Feeder's Diner here does not meet your definition of five-star dining?"

"The food was good, but I was talking about fine dining, wines, five-course meals, you know?"

"I am sure that Fred can prepare you a very tender rack of lamb with a sweet-glazed coating, and I'll do a flaming cherry jubilee for desert. How does that sound?" She was kind but was mocking Planner.

"Ms. Small, I am really trying to be quite serious."

She looked him over. "Sure, sure I have, the London Broil in Detroit before my son was born and then the Blue Stone and Rivercrest in Louisville."

"I have something for you to look at," Planner said, reaching over to the chair next to him to get his briefcase. "Would you mind taking a look at these plans?"

Somehow, maybe with an unseen eye in the back of her head, Becka sensed the couple approaching the register, excused herself, cashed out the couple, and returned in a matter of less than a minute.

"What are these?" she asked with a sense of curiosity.

"Blueprints of one of our establishments." Planner explained. "Would you mind if we spread them out?" He motioned to the recently toweled-off table.

She moved aside as the two men repositioned themselves at the table, the document now unrolled between them.

"I'd like your opinion, Ms. Small, on the layout for the restaurant," Sam stated.

Becka looked down for a moment at the blueprint, swiveled, and quickly retrieved the entrees for the last two customers in the restaurant, and again she stood over the table.

"I assume this is the floor plan for a restaurant, this being the dining area, this here the bus station, and here the kitchen." Becka pointed out various points on the print to ensure that she understood.

Planner nodded his head yes. "Actually, a detailed layout of the entire floor space."

"Who designed this?" she inquired.

"Why do you ask?" Mr. Price stated.

"Well, if I think I read this correctly, it is all wrong." She momentarily looked at Mr. Price with an inquisitive expression on her face. "Fine dining, right?" Her attention focused back on the large document spread across the table. "What seating for one hundred ten, maybe a hundred fourteen tops."

Planner nodded his head yes.

Becka reached behind her ear and removed the short pencil that she never used in writing down an order. "May I write on this?" she asked with her concentration focused intensely on what lay on the table.

Before either man could respond, Becka started sketching on the print. "This wall, that should be here. If you are serving fine food, why would you allow these three tables to have a clear view into the kitchen? No one wants to stay and enjoy a fine meal when they see all the activity in the kitchen. Those tables will go unused if you leave it like that." Her hand quickly scribbled out a new wall.

"And this angle here, if you move the double doors here and separate them with this type of pillar, you are going to avoid a lot of collisions, spills, and mishaps." She sketched in new doors on the print. "And the wait station, where are the bins for ice and maybe some shelving for glasses and a rack for wine glasses?" Her pencil breezed over the document.

"And look," she stated confidently, "three booths along this back wall and you gain seating for maybe four to six, and besides, there are plenty of couples who enjoy the intimacy of a booth. Maybe some alcoves here for some artwork. . ."

Becka seemed immersed in changing the design until she suddenly stood, refilled the last patrons' drinks, took and delivered a dessert order, and then returned to the table.

The little woman with the yellow blouse and the brown skirt stood over the document, the pencil juggled between two fingers on her left hand. "Who did you say drew this up?" she asked, not waiting for an answer and sitting down in a chair. "And look, if you reshape the kitchen this way, you can avoid running gas lines under the floor." Her pencil darted over the print, making both subtle and major changes.

She got up, met the last two customers at the register, and stepped back into the kitchen when she heard her named bellowed out by Fred.

Price looked at Planner. "Is she right?" His question was direct.

Planner looked over the prints, toward his boss, and back to the prints without answering.

Price knew what the answer would be. "Sam, how much would these changes have cost us if we had completed construction and wanted to redo it her way?"

Planner was embarrassed because he recognized that significant money would have been wasted. He fumbled for an amount. "Fifteen, maybe twenty thousand." He voiced out the words feebly.

"Get out the checkbook and pay her," Price stated.

"What?" Sam almost choked on the response.

"You heard me, Sam. You're an architectural engineer in the restaurant business with, what, seven years of college, and this little lady turns these plans inside out."

Price was a tough but fair boss. He forced a smile in Planner's direction as Sam reached into his briefcase and obtained a checkbook. "Make it out for twenty-five thousand dollars, Sam."

Planner gulped, knowing that his employer had every right to eventually take the money out of his fee.

Becka exited the kitchen and came back to the table, the nub of the pencil again in her hand and ready to be put to paper.

"Becka, would you take the time and go over the rest of the print with Sam here?"

"Sure," she stated but still seemingly anxious to put pencil to paper.

"I'll pay you—" Price's statement was cut off by her statement.

"You don't have to pay me anything for this, Mr. Price. I enjoyed the break." As she spoke, Sam slipped the folded check in front of her, but when she repositioned the blueprint, the check went unnoticed under the document.

"I don't want any money for this," she stated. "It's just that these changes would have—"

"How would you like to work for me, Becka?" Price asked bluntly.

"Well, I don't know," she responded. "Fred is really a good boss, and if I get enough shifts in, I can make some good money."

"How much?" Price's statement was again put bluntly.

She swallowed hard. "Two hundred fifty, maybe three hundred a week." She hedged to the high side. "But I'd want to work Friday and Saturday nights for the tips and maybe two weekdays off a week to be with my son."

Price was shaking his head no.

"One day a week off," she stated meekly.

"Becka, you don't understand. I want you to work with Sam here." He forced a smile in Planner's direction. "Goodness knows, maybe I should let him go and just hire you. No, I want you to help plan these sites and then set up—"

"Becka!" The gruff voice of Fred Feeder echoed out from the kitchen and cut through their conversation. "What am I paying you for? Get in here! You have to organize next week's order."

"Mr. Price, I got it pretty good here. Steady job, good tips, I could be doing a lot worse." The voice called out for her again. "Look, Fred is helpless unless I get the ordering done. If he did it, we'd all end up with nothing but ice cubes and paper cups."

"What if I leave this for you to read later, would that be all right?" Price's voice was almost begging her. "Take it home and look it over. I am sure we can work something out."

She nodded her head yes as she hustled toward the kitchen. "All you had was coffee, and that's on me, but the boss is a bellowing." She hurried back to the kitchen.

Becka had returned about fifteen minutes later, but Sam Planner and Mr. Price had left. A manila folder lay in the middle of the table with a folded check on top of it. What a way to leave a tip, she thought, as she slipped the check into the side pocket of her apron without looking at it and started to clear the last two tables in order to ready the restaurant for the evening clientele.

———————

Becka worked the long evening shift and headed home well after ten. She anticipated finding Richie up since it was a Friday night and found the lights on throughout most of the trailer when she arrived. She recognized that, at least, there was no heating bill to contend with at this time of year, but she would think that Richie could be a little more conservative with the electricity. She opened the still sticky front door and stepped inside and found Richie pulling on his shoes.

"I need to go for a walk before bed, Mom. Be back in a minute." He hugged her briefly and headed out into the yard and then around to the back of the trailer.

Her little boy put on a good face as to not being sad, but she knew differently. Through the circumstances that he had experienced, he was quickly becoming a young man. Yet each night before bed, there was that need to go outside and stand beside the grave of the dog he had loved and lost and try to control the pain that was still so present.

She went to the kitchen table and dropped her purse onto its surface. She remembered that she had carried the envelope that Mr. Planner and Mr. Price had given her home with her sweater and a box containing part of an apple pie. She stowed the pie in the refrigerator, hung the sweater on a peg over the washer, and stared at the still unopened envelope. Something she could look at later, she thought, it having been a busy day with almost the entire staff out sick.

As customary, she emptied her pockets of her tip money, placing the change on the counter and then gathering the dollar bills up to place in a jar well back on the top shelf. As she unfolded the money, the pale blue check, folded crisply in half, floated down onto the table. How much of a tip for two cups of coffee, she thought, as she reached over and tried to flatten the instrument. Since she had no bank account, she realized that she should have cashed it out at the till at the diner. Still, she concluded, she could take it back the next day and exchange the check for cash.

Her eyes momentarily focused on the check, and she saw the number two, then a five, then a zero, and then more zeroes. She pushed the paper flat on the kitchen table. On the check, she saw her name, Rebecca Small, and then the figure of twenty-five thousand dollars. Her chest seemed like it could neither expand nor contract as if there was no need to breathe. Twenty-five thousand dollars for what? she thought.

She looked at the manila folder still sitting on the table. At first, she was fearful of opening it and then reached across and flipped open the clasp, holding it shut.

The contract was simply stated—an opportunity to help in the design, staffing, training, and operation of restaurants at both the mall and the resort. The amount of the monthly salary was staggering to her, more money in a week than she could earn in a year at Fred Feeder's Friendly Diner. Tears began to dwell up in her eyes, big tears that gushed down her cheeks and then onto the document in front of her. She started to sob because she had thought about all the hard times, the times when she did not know how she could pay for the heat, gas for the car, or food for just two people. And across the document in ink was scrawled an addition to the contract with the signature of I.M. Price. It simply stated that she would be required to take off two days per week.

Richie opened the door and took off his damp shoes and then noticed that his mother was in tears. "Mother, are you okay? Is something wrong?" Richie ran to her mother.

She could not answer and just hugged him for the longest moment, tears still running down her face.

"Mother, what is it? Please don't cry." Richie was starting to panic as she pushed the document and the check across the table toward him.

He looked at the document, then the check, and then back at his mother. "Mom, we're rich!"

Becka Small was emphatically shaking her head no. Then as she quelled some of the tears, she finally spoke. "No, Richie, no, my dear. We were always rich. We always had each other, and that is what made us wealthy." She hugged him hard. "Now, now. . ." Her voiced cracked. "Now we will have enough to be comfortable."

CHAPTER 27

I T WAS A warm summer day. Richie lay out in the backyard with the Volume S of the *World Book Encyclopedia*. The original set his mother had obtained at a garage sale had been lacking volumes B, R, and S. But now with her new job and the additional money, she had purchased him a brand-new set, a full set. He had already learned about baseball, Brazil, and bees, about radios, Rangoon, and Ronald Regan. Now he was in the S volume and deeply immersed in the topic of salt.

It had been almost ten weeks since Lady had died, and the time involved in healing was changing the open wounds of grief into less obvious scars. He still found it necessary to come and sit by the grave. Sometimes he would just sit and stare out into the now growing stalks of corn. On other occasions, he would remember and then try to forget by enjoying his passion for reading.

Becka was now working for Mr. Price. She worked hard but earned an excellent salary. And the required two days off a week meant that she and Richie could be together, even take trips in the recently purchased almost new automobile, and make plans for the house they were going to build in the lot next to the trailer.

Richie too was changing. He was slowly relinquishing the morbid solitude that had consumed him for so many weeks. Tyrone, Carl, Ben, and the others treated him like both a brother and a member of the club, and that had helped. But it was time that had brought about much of the healing.

Then there was his new friend. Clarence Goodfellow made it a point to ride his bike over and spend time talking and trying to joke with Richie. On many occasions, he would grow quiet, stop, and stare out at what Richie was observing, silent, except for the gigantic tears that would spill over his still round cheeks and drop with a silent thud into his lap. His bicycle seat was no longer taking such a beating since he had lost thirty pounds in less than three months. The reason for his monumental efforts was simple—he desired to be more like Richie.

And of course, there was Tina. They spent hours together sitting and reading or walking into town, words often not necessary for them to communicate. Time just spent outside talking about Lady or the comfort of knowing that they both felt the flutter of that trapped bird in the middle of their chest when they were together. She had become someone special to him, and he really did not know why, but those birds always fluttered about inside when she was near.

Clarence Goodfellow was the first to arrive. He parked his bike off to the side of the driveway and walked around back to find his friend.

"Hi, RJ," he stated. "What are you reading?"

Richie looked up at his new friend. "Salt, all about salt."

Then Tina and her father appeared, followed by Tyrone, Carl, and Ben and then his mother with her new friends, Bob and Carol Learner.

"Mom, what are you doing home?" He looked about with suspicion, knowing something was going on, and saw Dr. Wild and the woman from East Lansing that he had met ten weeks earlier named Jennifer. In his arms, Dr. Wild held a large brown box that seemed to have a life of its own, as if it wanted to squirt from the clutches of his arms.

"Richard, remember me, Dr. Jennifer Cares from Michigan State?"

Richie nodded his head yes.

The pretty young veterinarian came and stood next to him. Last fall, he would have had to look up at her, but in the eight months that had passed, the growth spurt of almost five inches now placed him almost in eye-to-eye contact.

"I haven't been honest with you, Mr. Small," she said. "A while ago, I did something that I should have told you about, but I did not. I was wrong in thinking that you might not able to handle it, but there was so little chance that they would survive and that I would be here today."

Dr. Wild placed the box on the ground and tipped it toward one side. Three small Labradors spilled over the edge—a chocolate and yellow male and an even smaller yellow female. Immediately, the two males pounced on each other and stumbled their way over the thick grass, one finally rolling right over its head and lying with its bare belly pointing toward the sky while biting at the ear of the chocolate straddling him.

"These are your puppies, Lady's puppies," Dr. Wild said.

"No, they are not." Richie spoke directly into the face of Jennifer.

"They are, Richard. Lady struggled all night until they were born. The others died, but these three, through a sort of miracle and with the help of a cat, they're here ten weeks later."

She touched him softly on the shoulder. "They are probably closer to six weeks old because they were so premature." She turned toward the dogs and then back to him. "And they are healthy and full of energy, and they are yours."

Richie looked over at the animals as the two males tumbled and rumbled through the grass, one giving out a high-pitched yelp while sprawled over the other. The female seemed to ignore them both and wandered through the grass, looking around and sniffing at the air.

"What if I don't want them?" Richie looked at Dr. Wild and Jennifer. The death of Lady, the death of any dog was something Richie never wanted to face again.

"Well, they are yours to do with what you want. You can give them to someone, or we will take them back and find them a good home," Dr. Wild answered.

"Clarence, he can have the chocolate one," Richie said bluntly. "And Tina, she can have the yellow. That way, they will live in the same neighborhood until, at least, Mr. Price finishes their house." Richie pointed in the direction of the two playful males.

"And the little one"—Richie turned to find the female—"give her to. . ."

The little dog had wandered to the mound where her mother was buried and pawed gently at the newly planted grass. She seemed to look up at the wooden marker that

Clarence's dad had made with Lady's name etched under the clear varnish on the wood. Then she turned, looked at Richie, and tilted her head and pricked up her ears as if studying only Richie. Her dark black eyes locked on him as she moved closer to him and sniffed at his shoelaces and licked the sock over his ankle. She sat at the toe of his shoe and looked back over at the marker and then up at him.

"What could I name her?" Richie meekly spoke out the words.

Becka touched her son on his shoulder, which was now above her own. "Why don't you name her Lady? I don't think that Lady would mind."

Richie fell to his knees and gently rubbed his fingers over the dog's raised head. They would be almost inseparable for the next fifteen more years.

CHAPTER 28

THE TWO WOMEN had listened intently as the young woman finished talking. They had sat there for over two hours hearing the story, finally ready for the services that their animals could provide as leader dogs. The two female yellow Labrador Retrievers had lain calmly at their feet, prepared to be the eyes for their now masters and allowing them opportunities in their lives that may not have been possible six weeks earlier.

"Your two dogs are the descendants of the first Lady," the young woman in the room stated. "Generations and generations of Lady's descendants have passed through this school and have been the most successful of our leader dogs."

She had paused, and the two women heard her take a long breath. Blind people were perceptive in ways that did not involve sight, and they realized that the person telling the story had been emotionally drained as if directly involved in all that had been said.

"Whatever happened to Richie, Richie Small?" the woman asked.

"He is a doctor, a pediatrician with offices in Bloomfield Hills, Michigan. He specializes in childhood diseases and is one of the best in his field in the entire country.

"Why didn't he become a veterinarian?" the other woman inquired.

"Because he could never completely forget about Lady. He just could not bring himself to work with sick animals."

"And Becka, is she still working for Mr. Price?" the other asked.

"Well, sort of," the young woman answered with a chuckle. "I guess you could say he is working for her. After opening numerous restaurants, training and staffing them, and overseeing their operation, she finally gave in to his pursuing her. They were married just over six years ago."

"How about Tyrone, Tyrone Walker?" both women chimed in.

"He played football for Eureka Springs. In fact, they won the state championship that very next year. It was the first of, I think, seven championships that Head Coach Learner has had. Coach Ball left that very year that Lady died. His wife still teaches fifth grade, and Coach Learner is commander at the state police post over in Traverse City. They have two boys now too, two strapping young boys of their own."

"And Tyrone went on to play football?" One of the women voiced the statement as a question.

The young woman was nodding her head yes as she answered, even though she could not be seen. "He played at Alabama, an all-American running back, and signed a professional contract with the Oakland Raiders. He was injured during his third professional season."

"That is too bad," one of the women stated sadly.

"For football maybe but not for us because Ty runs one of the largest minority-owned financial management companies in the country. In fact, this wing of the facility was built with a contribution from him and his wife." The young woman's smile went unobserved by the two women. "His wife, the former Sarah Beamer, is very involved with the school. It would seem that she, along with Richard and Mrs. Learner, did a good job in teaching him to read."

A smile had also spread across one of the blind women's face. "May I dare ask about Clarence?"

"Clarence." The young woman chuckled. "One of the key linemen on a couple of Coach Learner's championship teams and went on to play at Michigan State. In fact, he was a tackle during Richard's freshmen and sophomore years. Now he is teaching in Eureka Springs and is Coach Learner's assistant. Richard credits him with his all-Big Ten seasons his sophomore and junior years."

"Richie played?" one of the women asked.

"Just three years. He ended up playing outside line-backer and starred on Michigan State's two Big Ten championship teams," the young woman responded. "He. . ." She stumbled with the words. "I entered the veterinarian program at Michigan State during the beginning of my junior year. Richard transferred to the medical school at the University of Michigan at the beginning of his senior year and gave up football to begin medical school early."

One woman stood and approached the speaker. Somehow, she reached out and touched the young woman's face, knowing exactly where she sat, as if seeing. Gently she reached out and passed her fingertips over the right eyebrow of the speaker, and the young woman did not object.

"You are Tina." The woman made the comment with a certain reverence.

"Yes, yes, I'm Tina, now Mrs. Tina Small," she responded. "But there is no scar. My father's money took care of that." The young woman again hesitated. "You both are very lucky to have dogs like Sandy and Penny."

At the mention of their names, the two animals pricked up their ears, tilted their heads, and looked at the speaker.

"No," one of the women stated. "You, my dear, you and Richard are the lucky ones."

Tina Small rose to leave, and the two women and the two dogs sensed it. "One last question." the woman next to Penny faced where Tina stood. "Did anyone ever find out where Lady came from?" The woman's statement somehow lacked the form of a question.

She had been asked that question numerous times before, and after all these years, it still remained unanswered.

After a long an awkward silence, the blind woman with her first seeing eye dog simply stated, "Who says angels have to have wings."

A smile ran across the pretty doctor's face. "No one, no one at all."

ABOUT THE AUTHOR

CRAIG GEORGEFF SPENT thirty-six years as a special agent with the federal government and conducted numerous investigations in Northern Michigan. The inspiration for this book comes from his wife, Carol, who taught reading for thirty years in a community much like the village described in this book. And living with a dedicated teacher means hearing and knowing about all their students, their successes, and their failures. Carol encouraged the writing of this book to challenge readers of any age to share in a passion for the written word before losing her battle with cancer. Craig still resides in mid-Michigan and extensively travels the state from Lake Michigan to Lake Huron and north to the cold waters of Lake Superior. Occasionally, he slips South to Florida and Texas to visit friends and family.